★

Fonnie gained control over her emotions, angrily wiped the tears out of her eyes. "You need to call Mike Dickson. This has something to do with Christine Hauner's murder."

Three policemen stared at Fonnie, their eyes puzzled, their mouths partially open. Dwayne broke the silence. "You knew the murdered woman?"

"She worked for me. She had incriminating evidence against somebody. She blackmailed him or her. Then she changed her mind and was killed. But she hid the evidence. That's what they were after. They think she hid it here. It's all very clear now."

Brian walked Fonnie over to the sofa and sat down with her. He placed his hands on his grandmother's shoulders. "It's not clear at all. You know nothing of the kind. You're imagining all this."

Tyrone stepped forward from where he'd been standing in the far corner. "She may be right. It makes sense."

 ★

Previously published Worldwide Mystery title by
HELEN GOODMAN

MURDER IN EDEN

TOXIC WASTE

HELEN GOODMAN

W🌐RLDWIDE®

TORONTO • NEW YORK • LONDON
AMSTERDAM • PARIS • SYDNEY • HAMBURG
STOCKHOLM • ATHENS • TOKYO • MILAN
MADRID • WARSAW • BUDAPEST • AUCKLAND

In loving memory of my son, Ronnie

TOXIC WASTE

A Worldwide Mystery/July 2008

First published by Alabaster Books.

ISBN-13: 978-0-373-26642-5
ISBN-10:   0-373-26642-1

Printed in U.S.A.

Acknowledgments

Special thanks to my critique group: Nancy Gates, Wendy Greene, Diane Berry, Dorothy O'Neill, and Betty DiMeo.

Thanks also to members of the Triad Writers Roundtable: Dixie Land, Larry Jakubsen, David Shaffer, Joanne Clarey, Kathy Fisher, John Staples, Lynette Hampton, and Emogene Joyner.

PROLOGUE

THE CLAWING AND SCRAPING at the kitchen door went on for several minutes before the door crashed open. Two slight figures invaded the room. They were dressed in the teen uniform of Carolina streets: faded jeans with waistlines plunging close to indecency, black tee shirts, and logo-covered caps worn backwards. One cap touted the Carolina Panthers while the other one extolled a NASCAR driver. The boys knew the house was empty so they made no attempt to hide their faces: innocent, suntanned faces, too young to shave, one even too young to drive.

Their eyes followed the glow from the flashlight as it crept across the linoleum and as it swung around the big country kitchen. It landed on cane-back chairs around a table covered with a red and white oilcloth. "Hey," the younger boy said. "This looks like your granny's kitchen. Who lives here?"

"Some old gal. In a nursing home now. Ain't never coming back. Come on. Let's find something worth taking."

They headed into the dining room. The light paused as it landed on the china cabinet.

"Reckon those fancy dishes are worth anything?" The high-pitched wobbly voice echoed through the room, bounced off the chandelier.

"Naw," the older boy answered in a deeper, steadier tone. "Besides, we can't get bogged down carrying a bunch of dishes. What we want is some good silver stuff. Stuff that's easy to hock." He shined the light on a lowboy across the room. "Check those drawers over there."

The younger boy did as he was told. He opened and shut drawers until he let out a whoop. "He-e-e-y. Lookie here." The drawer stuck a little and the boy jerked wildly. As he did, the drawer and its contents banged to the floor. Silver knives and forks and spoons and serving pieces scattered at the boy's feet.

"Be quiet, you fool," the older boy said. "You want the whole neighborhood to hear?"

"But you said the neighbors were gone. Didn't you say they were gone?"

"Yeah, they're gone, but there's still no use you making enough racket to wake the dead. Let's bag this stuff and get out of here." He yanked a cloth tote bag out of his pocket and both boys started grabbing and shoving. Soon silverware, stuck every which way, gorged the bag.

"This will bring big bucks," the older boy said. He let out a slight groan as he lifted the bag. "Man, this is heavy." He tossed the flashlight to the other boy. "Here, take this."

The younger boy took advantage of the flashlight to see more of the area. He brandished the streams of light through the archway, into the den, and onto a shelf of figurines. "Hey, what are those things?"

"What things?"

"Those crazy little animals on the shelf up there."

The other boy shifted the weight of the silverware and stared at the shelves. The light waved back and forth. There were horse-like figures of all sizes, each with a single horn projecting from its forehead. Some were of wood, some of glass, some of various metals.

"Don't you know nothing?" the older boy said. "They're unicorns. They lived a long time ago—like dinosaurs. They're all dead now. But I think they were supposed to be lucky or something like that."

The younger boy giggled. "They weren't too lucky if they all up and died." He wiggled the light again and the beam fell on a shiny six-inch-tall silver unicorn rearing up on his hind legs.

The older boy dropped the bag for a moment. "That one's silver. I think I'll take him for myself." He reached up, snatched the silver unicorn from the shelf, tossed him into the bag. "Now let's go."

ONE

October 5

I'm scared. It's a new feeling for me. Even when I had my stroke I wasn't scared. Depressed? Yes. But not scared. I knew I would either die or learn to cope. Dying would have been easier, but instead, I coped. It hasn't been simple. Physical therapy is brutal, but I've made progress. My doctor says I don't need to be at Springwillow now. I've gone from a wheelchair to a quad cane. I can shuffle down the hall. And with Velcro, I can pretty much dress myself. But am I really ready to go home?

And the worst thing about being afraid is I can't tell anybody. I have my public persona to protect. I'm the invincible Fonnie Beachum, next in line to the unsinkable Mollie Brown. But surely even Mollie had her periods of self doubt, her "monsters under the bed" moments.

FONNIE STUDIED THE COMPUTER screen; she glanced over her left shoulder to be sure no one had come up behind her. The room was empty except for the row of monitors with their multicolored screen savers waiting to commune with other lonely souls. Several months ago she'd started keeping a journal. Brian had suggested it.

"It'll be good for you, Gram. Just write whatever comes into your head. It's like having your own private shrink, except instead of lying on a sofa, you can spill your guts to the computer."

"And this is supposed to save my sanity?"

"Well," Brian said, giving her a big grin. "Maybe not save it, but it'll make losing your mind more interesting."

So every few days Fonnie wheeled herself, or more recently, shuffled her way to the computer room. She had no grand plan for her writing. She wrote whatever was gnawing at her brain or her heart or her guts on any particular day. It was rather slow going since she still had limited use of her left hand, but time meant little to her here. At the end of each session, Fonnie printed out the page and slipped it into a folder. Then she carefully deleted it from the screen. Fonnie had only recently become acquainted with computers, and although she delighted in getting e-mail and browsing the web, she didn't intend to leave details of her private life etched on any hard drive or floppy disc.

Fonnie refocused on the computer screen and what she'd just written. She knew the root of her fear. A few months ago her house had been burglarized. The back door was jimmied and her silverware stolen. She didn't even know about it until Brian moved in. He'd returned to Groverton after college to join the police force. He found the silverware drawer on the floor of the dining room—empty. Her home, her life, had been violated. No trace of her silverware had been found in any of the nearby pawnshops. No one had been caught. What if it happened again?

Brian assured her it wouldn't. He installed deadbolt locks on all the doors and added some outdoor lighting.

The house was secure. Now she had only to secure her mind against the shadowy fear.

She *did* want to go home. And she wouldn't be alone. Brian would be there. Officer Brian Hendley—it sounded rather grand. He was still in rookie training, inundated with work and study, but he would be in and out of the house. And her social worker had requested a home health aide for her—three hours a day, five days a week. Fonnie understood the arrangement was temporary, only until she became more independent. Since she was a retired nurse, she knew how closely insurance companies monitored the use of resources. But even if she just had the aide for thirty days, it would get her over the hump of being home and being on her own.

Mary Scoggins, the nurse from the Family Home Health Agency had visited Fonnie yesterday to assess her needs. "I have just the aide for you," she said. "Her name is Christine Hauner. I'm sure you'll find her satisfactory."

BRIAN SLOWED THE CAR as he turned right off East Sixth Street onto Mimosa Lane. The lone mimosa tree left on the block waved its nearly barren limbs at Fonnie as they neared her house. Her mind tried to conjure up its summer, salmon-pink blossoms she'd loved through the years. It was hard to do with the new Radio Shack crouching close by flashing its red neon light. The commercial district, fast encroaching on the neighborhood, routinely replaced trees with parking lots and birds' songs with ringing cash registers.

"I see there are more vacant houses," she said. "I hate to see the young families moving out."

"You can't blame them. The suburbs are nicer, better schools, safer."

"I know, but I'll miss the happy squeals of children, the barbeque aromas, even the weekend din of lawn-mowers." Fonnie reached across with her right hand and patted Brian's arm. "But I feel perfectly safe with you living with me."

When the white clapboard two-story house came into view, she rolled down the car window. The house had been built when this part of the county was still semi-rural. Through the years it had been enlarged and modernized, but it still retained its comfortable farm-house facade.

The late afternoon sun sank behind the house leaving deepening shadows. Fonnie felt an unexpected shiver of foreboding. She thrust her uneasiness to the back of her brain, turned, and nodded to Brian. "It's good to be home."

She could tell that Brian had done his best to make her homecoming a festive occasion. He tied red and yellow balloons to the front porch railing, and draped a computer-generated banner reading *Welcome Home* over the doorway.

Fonnie was touched, but she knew Brian didn't want any sloppy sentiments. "What? No brass band? It isn't every day a conquering hero comes marching home."

Brian ambled around the car, opened her door and helped her out. He held her left arm as she got her footing and balanced on her cane. She teetered slightly going up the steps, smiled when she reached the top. "Another mountain conquered."

Brian stretched his six-foot frame an inch taller, stuck a thumb under his belt, wiggled it around. "I just hope this conquering hero hasn't forgotten how to cook. Because I'm wasting away like a shriveled carrot stick."

"Is that why you were so anxious to bail me out of

Springwillow? Well, I've got news for you. Until I get my sea legs back, my cooking will be limited to cereal and toast."

Brian laughed. He clasped Fonnie by the waist, kissed her on the cheek. "Welcome home, Gram. It's good to know you're still full of piss and vinegar."

"And I still have a good right hand, so you watch your mouth unless you want to feel the back of it."

"Yes'um." He helped her into the house and onto the den sofa. "Now you sit yourself down while I check your e-mail. You might have some messages from your many admirers. I moved my computer down here so you can use it anytime you like."

"Good." Fonnie was already mentally composing her next journal entry, *Home Sweet Home.*

Brian turned back to look at her. "You've got a short note from Mom. Want me to print it out?"

"Yes, please." She was anxious to see what Amy had written. Fonnie's relationship with her daughter had been strained the past few months because Fonnie encouraged Brian's interest in police work while Amy opposed it.

"A complete waste of your college education," Amy had told Brian one day when they were both visiting the nursing home. "Your economics degree has nothing to do with law enforcement. And why you want to come back to Groverton is beyond me. I don't even know why you want to stay in North Carolina. You could come up to Richmond; I could introduce you to some of my business friends; you could really make something of yourself."

Brian shrugged. "It's hard to explain. Richmond may be only a few hours away, but it's a different world.

Groverton is hardly Mayberry, but it still has a small-town feeling. And I like it." Brian gave his mother an impish grin and winked at his grandmother. "And I want to be a cop because I'll look great in my uniform. Gals will be flinging themselves at me."

To her credit, Amy had the grace to smile as she mussed his thick wavy blond hair. "Just wait until the cops give you a crew cut, or whatever they call it these days. Your gals will be brokenhearted once they can't run their fingers through your golden locks."

"Guess I'll just have to rely on my wit and charm."

Fonnie smiled at the memory. Brian had an abundance of both. It was going to be so good to have him living with her.

He handed her the e-mail. Brisk and businesslike, just like Amy, Fonnie thought, no salutation, no amenities.

Sorry I couldn't be there to help with your move, but I'm sure Brian can handle everything. He told me he was going to take the entire day off. I'll call you next week after you've had time to get settled and rested.

Later that evening after a Papa John's pizza, Fonnie stretched out on the sofa and pulled the granny-square afghan over her legs. She closed her eyes for a short nap. It was good to be home. She was beginning to feel warm and snug and safe.

When she awoke, her gaze went to the shelf containing her collection of unicorns. It took a few moments for the empty space to register in her brain, but when it did, Fonnie sat straight up, tossed aside the afghan, and let out a bellow. "Brian. Come here. Now!"

Brian sprinted down the open staircase, did a quick

right turn into the den, and stared wide-eyed at his grandmother. "What's wrong? Are you sick? Didn't that pizza agree with you?"

Fonnie sat there shaking her right hand at something across the room. "That's what's wrong. Leopold is missing!"

Brian swiveled around, his eyes following her pointing fingers, then turned back in bewilderment. "Who is Leopold?"

"My silver unicorn. He always stood in the middle of the bottom shelf. And he's gone. Have you been messing with my collection?"

"No ma'am. I haven't touched your unicorns. I learned better than that when I was three. You spanked me for climbing up on a chair just to look at them."

"Has anybody else been in the house?"

"I hired a cleaning service last week to come in and spiff up the place. I thought you might not like two inches of dust on everything. But they're bonded, and I was here with them most of the time. If they were going to steal something, I'm sure it would be something more valuable than a toy unicorn."

Fonnie squeezed her eyes shut to keep back the tears. She no longer felt snug and safe. Leopold might seem like a toy to Brian and perhaps to anyone else, but to Fonnie that particular mythical beast was a symbol of love and security. Harrison gave it to her for their first anniversary. It was the start of her collection. Through the years, Leopold was joined by unicorns of every size and description, but Fonnie always loved him the best; he was the only one she'd given a name.

Brian studied the empty space. "I guess it could have

been stolen when your silverware was taken and I just didn't notice. Sorry."

Brian looked so dejected, Fonnie attempted a smile for him. "That's probably what happened. Nothing to be done about it now."

Brian turned to go back upstairs. "I've better get back to my studying."

Fonnie knew she was being silly, but Leopold's disappearance shook her sense of security. She felt a nebulous fear creeping over her.

TWO

BEBE ENGLEHOOK drove down West Sixth Street, past the new Super Wal-Mart, past Discount City, slowed as she approached Burger Castle, turned into Hawthorne Drive. The drive zigzagged past West Side High School and the Heavenward Gospel Church. She pulled the wine-colored extended cab pickup into the driveway between the church and the parsonage, and stopped at a slate-gray building in back.

The building was part tool shed, part carpenter shop, and part artist studio, all of it ruled over by sixteen-year-old Tyrone Riggs. Bebe glanced at her watch. She hoped she wasn't too early. She knew Tyrone didn't get home from school until three-thirty. It was now just after four. Maybe he hadn't had time to finish the signs yet, but Bebe was anxious to find out.

Exiting the truck was never an easy task for Bebe since she was barely five feet two inches tall. She first had to plant one foot securely on the door rim, then clutch the back of the seat while her other foot closed the distance between cab and ground. When she was younger, it wasn't much of a problem, but the further she got into her fifties, the harder it became. Some days her increasingly arthritic joints clamored for a nice low-slung sedan. So far she had resisted trading. She needed the truck, especially now.

Bebe heard hammering coming from the building and knocked loudly. A big, brown, smiling hunk, wearing a paint-splattered sweat shirt, opened the door. "Hello, come in. Just finishing up."

Bebe watched Tyrone pound the last nail into the last sign, just under the letter P. He propped it up on its one leg next to the others, and waited for her word of approval. It wasn't long in coming. "They're great. You're a real artist."

"I know. Too bad I have to waste my time painting protest signs."

"Waste your time? You don't realize how important this demonstration is. We've alerted the media, the county commissioners, the Environmental Protection Agency. This is big. It may well be the end of Myerson's venture in Groverton County. Are you sure you have enough signs?"

"I contracted for forty-five signs. I made forty-five signs. Fifteen each. Count them yourself."

Bebe strolled down the line of signs, each one painted in blood red letters on a dandelion-yellow background. They were stacked in three different piles, each with their own message. Bebe nodded in satisfaction as she read the commands and counted the signs. STOP MYERSON. STOP THE POISON. STOP THE LANDFILL.

She paused in front of one Myerson sign. "Looks like you dribbled a little paint on this one. See those drops below the M?"

Tyrone smiled. "Actually I was enjoying a little artistic license on that one. If you look closely, you'll see that they represent drops of blood. Isn't that your point? That Myerson's landfill will poison the town and drain out our lifeblood?"

Bebe's dark eyes widened in admiration. She touched the red drops spilling out from her adversary's name. "Exactly." She picked up the sign, clutched it to her denim jacket. "This one's mine, and I'll make sure the TV cameras get a close-up view."

Bebe finished her inventory. "You must have counted wrong, Tyrone. You made an extra poison sign. There are sixteen instead of fifteen."

She contemplated the boy in front of her. Yes, he was still a boy in spite of the man's body. His eyes were innocent and happy, his smile impetuous. His voice held none of the anger or disillusionment many of his peers exhibited. He seemed to understand her anger toward the corporation bent on leeching Groverton, but it hadn't really touched his soul.

She decided to test him. "Or was that deliberate too? Did you make the sixteenth one for yourself ? Are you going to march with us?"

Tyrone shook his head. "I admit I considered it, but Pop wouldn't like it, and Keisha would have a hissy fit."

"Why?"

"Actually, Pop is in favor of the landfill. Some people in the church have tried to organize against it, but Pop says our town needs it, that Myerson has submitted all the required papers, environmental impact and all that, and it will benefit our community. There'll be some new jobs, the company will pay a lot of taxes, so it'll help everybody."

"And I guess you still believe in Santa Claus, too?"

"I didn't say I believed it. I was just telling you what my dad thought. He also thinks a minister's family ought to stay out of public controversy."

"I see. Times sure have changed since Martin Luther

King. What does your pop think about you making protest signs for a white rabble-rouser like me?"

"He wouldn't like it, but he doesn't know. I just told him my art teacher got me a job doing custom work for a civic organization." Tyrone flashed Bebe a grin. "But I didn't tell him that my teacher, Mr. Vincent, had a 'thing' for the leader of this organization and that he paid for the work."

Bebe's eyes opened wider at this bit of news. "Neil Vincent has already paid you for the work? And what do you mean, he has a 'thing' for me?"

"That's right. He said the payment was his contribution to the cause since he's not officially a member of the group. And he kept bragging on you and said he intended to march in the protest even though the school board wouldn't approve of it. My conclusion is that he likes you."

"Well, of course, he likes me. Neil and I have been friends for years, but that doesn't translate into anything more serious." Bebe picked up one of the signs. "Let's get going with these. I just hope your dad doesn't see us loading them into my truck."

"He won't. I got trash bags to put over each one—to protect the paint."

"Good." Bebe grabbed a black plastic bag and slipped it over her special sign—protecting the drops of blood. "By the way," she asked Tyrone, "who is this Keisha that you said would have a hissy fit if you joined the protest?"

"My big sister. The trouble is, she thinks she's my mother. Mom died about five years ago, and Keisha has been mothering me ever since."

"She agrees with your dad about the landfill?"

"I don't really know. I just know she keeps warning me about gangs, and she might call Citizens Against Toxic Waste At Groverton or CATWAG a gang."

Bebe laughed. "That's mild to *some* of the names we've been called."

THREE

October 13

> *Christine has been with me for a week now, and as Ms. Scoggins predicted, she is satisfactory. But on my grading scale, satisfactory translates to a C. And if she doesn't get here soon, her grade will be lowered to a C minus due to habitual tardiness.*
>
> *When I was working and had an eight o'clock start time, I always arrived by 7:55. It is now 8:05. This will be the third time she's come in late. She never even apologized or blamed it on traffic or fibbed about a broken alarm clock. In fact, she acted as if nothing was wrong. But today I'm going to set her straight.*

FONNIE PRESSED THE PRINT icon, got up from the computer, clutched her cane, and scuffled into the kitchen. She sipped her coffee and finished her bran flakes as she waited for Christine to arrive. She flipped on the kitchen counter TV. No need to get in a tizzy, she chided herself. She'd deal with Christine in due time.

The weatherman was confirming what Fonnie could see through her kitchen windows: temperature—fifty-two, light rain, gusty winds. She sighed as she watched the dappled, brownish-orange leaves make their annual descent back to earth. Their beauty should have been soothing to her soul. Instead, a line of poetry popped into her mind that was anything but soothing. It was a line from Robert Frost, *I'll only stop to rake the leaves away.* She forgot the next line but remembered the last words, *You come too.*

"But I can't go," Fonnie complained to her coffee cup. "I can't rake leaves ever again. I can't play in the leaves. All I can do is look at them. And it's not enough." She wallowed in self pity for a minute before turning her thoughts back to the morning news.

The anchorman was interviewing Dale Myerson, the president of Myerson Corporation. The proposed landfill controversy had been on the news and in the papers for weeks now, with both sides declaring their own views and condemning those of their opponents. Fonnie had taken little interest. She had enough to worry about in her own little world without being much concerned with social issues. But this was the first time she'd seen Mr. Myerson himself.

Always before, a Ms. Lanie Franklin had been the spokesperson for the corporation. The matter must be getting more serious to bring in the president of the company. Fonnie noticed that Ms. Franklin was seated off to one side. She was an African-American of indeterminate age, tall, big boned, dressed in a magenta suit and a floppy black hat. Fonnie smiled. Lanie Franklin may have been sidelined, but she wasn't going to be ignored. She was flanked by two of the county commissioners who had backed the landfill: Ed Whitehall and Gregory Fanning. Fonnie had never met either of the commissioners, but she knew their faces from frequent public appearances.

Mr. Myerson was speaking, and something about his voice caught Fonnie's attention. She knew the company's headquarters were in the eastern part of the state, the same area where Fonnie grew up. She'd moved away after high school and seldom went back to visit after her parents died.

She turned up the volume as Mr. Myerson spoke. "There's no question that Groverton County needs a new solidwaste landfill. The present landfill will reach its capacity within a few years. With the increase in manufacturing in the area and your new hospital, you're going to need more space. In addition, the new landfill will be large enough to accept solid waste from surrounding counties—at a charge, of course. And this revenue will be a welcome source of income to the county, which will allow your officials to offer more services to the citizens. It's really a win-win situation."

As the man talked on, something tugged at Fonnie's memory bank. There was an aura of familiarity about him: the wide forehead, the full lips, the easy smile, the way his smooth hands orchestrated his words. Of course—the memory slipped into place. Dale Myerson had been a schoolmate. He'd been a grade or two behind her, on the debate team, on the honor roll, and always surrounded by a gaggle of friends. Even at that young age he'd been a leader, someone who demanded and received attention. Fonnie wasn't surprised that he'd become the head of a company. He exuded self-assurance. Although not exactly handsome, his visage had an air of honesty and openness, and his words flowed softly, apparently without guile. Fonnie was pleased that a boy from her hometown had made good.

Mr. Myerson continued, "I simply don't understand

why a few people are stirring up so much controversy."
Fonnie wondered why also, and chided herself for not
being better informed.

The news reporter interviewing him interjected a
question. "But Mr. Myerson, how do you respond to the
charge made by the Citizens Against Toxic Waste At
Groverton that your proposed landfill may be hazardous
to the health of our citizens?"

Fonnie thought she detected a slight rolling of Dale's
eyes as he replied. "I'm sure the members of CATWAG,
as they call themselves, are fine, sincere people, but
they are mistaken in their allegations, and they are mis-
leading the other fine citizens of your city and county.
Incidentally, I think this group has chosen their acronym
well. These cats are busy wagging their tongues and
trying to sound like lions, but they have nothing to roar
about."

"But they report that, during a surprise inspection, the
state found twenty-seven violations on your trucks
hauling waste to one of your landfills in a neighboring
county. And that another one of your landfills shows
toxic mercury runoff in the rainwater. These sound like
rather serious problems."

Fonnie heard a rap on the kitchen door and called out,
"Come in." She glanced around as Christine meandered
in, slipped off her jacket, and hung it on the coat rack.
Fonnie held up her hand to forestall any conversation
until Dale gave his answer.

"Not serious at all. The reports of those inspections
are preliminary and are being challenged, as we speak,
by our company's attorneys. I can assure you that the
Myerson Corporation maintains and will continue to
maintain the highest safety standards in the industry."

The rest of his reply was muted by Christine's strident comment. "That's a bunch of baloney."

Fonnie swung around to face Christine. She was so surprised by Christine's remark that she forgot all about her planned lecture on tardiness. "What makes you say that?"

The nurse's aide seemed like such an ordinary person that Fonnie couldn't imagine her being a member of a radical group. She was middle-aged, a little plump, dull brown hair with a home-perm look, little makeup. She was the kind of person one could meet at a church function, trade pleasantries with, and then promptly forget. "Are you a member of CATWAG?" Fonnie asked.

Christine shook her head. "No, but I've been keeping up with the news, and they're right. Myerson can't be trusted."

"But we need a new landfill. What will the county do when the present one is full?"

A veil seemed to fall over Christine's face. She shrugged. "I really don't know anything about it. I shouldn't have said anything." She put her hands in her blue uniform jacket pockets. "Do you want me to get started on the dishes or run your bath first?"

ACROSS TOWN Bebe Englehook was watching the same TV interview. "The highest safety standards, my foot." She put the finishing touches on a report she was preparing to release to the media, citing multiple violations by the Myerson Corporation in several locations. She was convinced the only thing Myerson was concerned about was making a profit, and they did this by taking short cuts around or ignoring safety regulations. Bebe had organized CATWAG not to fight a new landfill, but to fight the corporation that had won the bid—a bid so low that the county commissioners had no choice but to accept it. A bid too low to ensure safety.

She made a note to call the TV station and demand equal time to present opposing views on Myerson. Bebe knew many people considered her a maverick, an activist looking for a cause. True, she'd supported a short-lived teacher strike when her children were in school. Most of the parents were appalled that the teachers would leave their classrooms to fight for higher pay. But Bebe knew the teachers were right in their demands, and she and her children marched right along with them. The teachers hadn't gotten all they asked for, but it was a step in the right direction. Another time, she'd joined a march of gun-control advocates. But now, with her children grown and her ex-husband long gone, Bebe lived alone, and most of the time she was just an ordinary, law-abiding citizen running her used-bookstore, Second Chance—and writing letters to the editor.

Lately, however, she'd been neglecting the bookstore, and next Monday she would close Second Chance for the day. On Monday, the day of the big protest, bulldozers would start work on the new landfill. Her plan was not to stop them, but to gain more media attention. All the CATWAGs would be there with their newly painted signs, joined by some recently recruited community-college students. And, if Tyrone had reported correctly, so would Neil Vincent.

Bebe's thoughts swirled around Neil for a few moments. What had he said to Tyrone for the boy to come to the conclusion that Neil's feelings for her were more than just friendship? And if that were true, how would she respond? Neil was already a widower when Bebe took an art class from him at the college. He was supplementing his high-school salary by teaching evening classes at the college. It turned out she had little aptitude for art, but they shared interests in community affairs and good literature. They would bump into each other at county commissioners' meetings, at school functions, and at book signings. Occasionally they would have coffee after a meeting and compare notes. She enjoyed his company, but he rarely talked about his personal life, and even more rarely inquired about hers. Maybe after this landfill mess ended, she'd try to get better acquainted with him.

Right now, though, Bebe had to keep focused on her immediate goal. She was determined to do anything that was necessary to stop the Myerson Corporation.

MONDAY MORNING dawned clear and cold. At the proposed landfill site, ice crystals clung to weeds and thorny brambles, and a thin layer of ice skimmed the scattered puddles. Bebe pulled off the gravel road and left her truck long before she reached the two parked bulldozers and the "No Trespassing" sign. She wanted to do everything legally today.

During the past few days she'd been in touch with the North Carolina Environmental Defense League. They'd promised to file a petition in Raleigh against the Myerson Corporation. They would charge that, "the proposed landfill would have a significant and adverse impact on the county's water quality, and that leachate from the landfill could not be safely handled by the existing waste-water treatment plant." However, the attorneys for the league had stressed the necessity for CATWAG to keep their demonstration legal and peaceful.

Bebe had called a strategy meeting the evening before.

They were to carry their signs and march around quietly. They were to make sure the TV cameras caught all the action, but in no way were they to defy the police. This demonstration was not only to show their protest, but to garner more support for the movement.

Bebe climbed into the back of her pickup to be ready to pass out the signs to the demonstrators. It was then she noticed a dark maroon SUV parked on the other side of the road nearly hidden in a thicket of scrub pines. She recognized the vehicle, but it appeared to be empty. She shaded her eyes against the morning sun and searched for the driver. She saw him near the barbed wire fence. What was Neil doing there? Planning on climbing over? Or worse yet, had he already been trespassing? More trucks and cars started arriving, followed closely by several police cars and TV vans. The noise of the traffic must have caught Neil's attention because he moved away from the fence. He looked up, saw Bebe, waved at her, and crossed the road. "Hi," he said, "looks like we're going to have quite a turnout."

Bebe returned his smile with a frown. "Neil Vincent, what on earth were you doing over there? We don't want anyone to accuse us of trespassing."

Neil gave her an innocent stare. "I wasn't trespassing. I just wanted to gauge the lay of the land. Come on, let's get these signs unloaded."

Bebe carefully removed the black bags and started handing signs down to Neil. Soon they were joined by fellow CATWAGs and students. The police cars drove past and parked near the gate leading to the landfill site. Two long, black Cadillacs came next. Bebe recognized these as Myerson's corporate cars. She watched Ms. Lanie Franklin, nattily dressed in khaki trousers and a

navy pea jacket, step out of one of them. With her was
Ed Whitehall, the county commissioner who had
become a top defender of the Myerson Corporation.
They were joined, from the other car, by two gentlemen
that Bebe couldn't name, but she assumed they were
company lawyers.

Bebe breathed deeply of the frigid air, smiled encour-
agement to the CATWAGs, and said to the world, "Let
the fun begin." She lifted her sign with the dripping
drops of blood and led the way toward the bulldozers.
She was followed by nearly fifty stern-faced, determined men and women, marching slowly, and silently
waving their signs.

The police officers kept wary eyes on the protesters,
but made no move to stop them. Ms. Franklin and her
companions flanked the "No Trespassing" sign on the
fence leading to the landfill site. Two men dressed in
heavy thermal jackets revved up the bulldozers. TV
cameras started to roll, capturing CATWAG's messages
for the rest of the county to see. STOP THE LAND-
FILL. STOP THE POISONING. STOP MYERSON.
The signs would be marching through thousands of
dens and living rooms that evening.

The police allowed Bebe and her followers to march
around unmolested for nearly ten minutes. Then Bebe
noticed Lanie Franklin nodding her head to the men on
the bulldozers. The machines started to move. Bebe
halted the marchers, and they formed a double line
facing the earth-moving equipment headed their way.
The bulldozers crept along, but the CATWAGs stood
their ground. The lawyers leaned over and said something to the Myerson vice-president. Ms. Franklin
nodded and motioned to the policeman in charge.

Bebe smiled as Sergeant Vic Helms came up to her. She and Vic had known each other for years, had kids the same age, and Vic's wife was a regular customer at her bookstore. "Good morning, Bebe. How are things with you?"

"Fine, thank you, and with you?"

"Not bad. Good turnout today."

"Yes. Like our new signs?"

"Very nice. But I guess it's about time to stash them away and let these people get on with their work. Don't want any trouble now."

"Of course. I think we've made our point. And our next confrontation will be in court." Bebe gestured to her group, and they started an orderly march back to her truck. As they carefully placed their signs in the back of the pickup, the bulldozers picked up speed, went through the gate, and headed for a low hillock. Bebe watched them until they were out of sight and the noise of their motors diminished slightly. If she hadn't had the court date to look forward to, she would have been bitterly disappointed. But, she thought, with the Environmental Defense League on our side, we may soon have a court order that will stop Myerson in his tracks.

Bebe opened her truck door, and was about to hoist herself up when she became aware of a strange silence. Surely the bulldozers couldn't be out of hearing range already, she thought. She looked around. Others seemed to have noticed it as well. Ms. Franklin and Mr. Whitehall hurried over to the police line where a conference seemed to be going on.

Just then the bulldozer sound started again. Bebe soon realized it was coming closer rather than going away. In a few moments one of the machines came back into sight, running much faster than when it had left.

Once at the gate, the driver slammed on the brakes, jumped down, and bolted over to the policemen. The man was shouting something, but Bebe couldn't make out what it was. Sergeant Helms listened, got on his radio, then gave instructions to the other officers. He motioned the bulldozer driver into his police car and they drove off in the direction the dozer had come from.

Bebe vaulted back down to the ground and joined dozens of others, including the TV cameramen, who were surging over to the gate to find out what was happening. A young policeman held up his hands to halt the advancing crowd. "I'm sorry. Orders are not to let anyone go any further."

Questions came from every direction. "What's going on?" "Someone hurt?" "What did the driver say?" "Where's the other bulldozer?"

The young policeman shook his head. "I can't tell you anything now."

Bebe found herself being pushed back toward Ms. Franklin. Bebe tried to maneuver around her when she saw the woman grab Mr. Whitehall's arm. "Omigawd," Bebe heard Lanie Franklin gasp. "Did you hear that?"

Mr. Whitehall shook his head. "I couldn't make out what was said. But it looks like something crazy is going on."

"I heard him say they found someone," Ms. Franklin told him. "A body, is what he said." Her usual commanding voice trembled. "What do you think he meant? A dead body?"

FONNIE FINISHED her third cup of coffee and glared at the clock as the hour hand glided toward nine. She rehearsed the "punctuality" speech she would deliver to

Christine the moment the aide stepped through the door. A few minutes late was one thing, but a whole hour became ridiculous. Fonnie was debating with herself whether to report the tardiness to the Home Health Agency that employed Christine when the phone rang. "Maybe that's her now," Fonnie said to the empty kitchen. She lifted her right hand, grasped the rubber handle of her cane, and pushed up with her right foot as the therapist had taught her. She rose, started toward the phone. In her hurry to stop the shrill ringing, she began to wobble dangerously. She reached out her left hand, steadied herself against the counter. The phone rang twice more before she could let loose of her cane and pick it up.

"Gram. Why don't you have the phone on the table like I told you to?"

"How do you know I don't? And whatever happened to your cheery 'good morning'?"

"I'm sorry. Things are kind of hectic around here. And I know you don't have the phone near you because you took too long to answer." Brian paused and his voice softened. "But Gram, before I say anything else, I want you to take the phone, go back over to the table and sit down."

Fonnie sensed an introduction to bad news, so she did as she was told. She knew no amount of protest or procrastination could change whatever was coming. She tucked the cordless phone under her left arm, grabbed her cane, stumbled back to the table. "All right. I'm ready."

Fonnie could hear her grandson breathing, but he didn't say anything. Fonnie's voice quivered. "What's happened?"

"I'm at the police station. Just got back from the demonstration at the new landfill site."

"Did it turn ugly? Was somebody hurt?" Fonnie's voice betrayed the frustration she was feeling. "So, tell me already."

"They found a body."

Brian hesitated.

"A body?"

"Yes. Christine Hauner's body."

FOUR

FONNIE CAUGHT HER BREATH, stared out the window. The wind had picked up. Leaves writhed and wrestled, tossed down without mercy. She was watching the death of a season at the same time she was hearing of another death.

Fonnie knew she had to say something. Brian was waiting for her response. First she had to verify exactly what he had said. "Christine? My Christine? Are you sure? You only met her one time."

"We're sure. She had ID on her and she was also identified by someone in the group."

"But Christine told me she wasn't a member of the protest group. What was she doing there?"

"We don't know too much at this point. And I really can't say anything else. I just wanted to let you know. I'll check with the home health agency and have another aide sent out."

Fonnie shook her head at the telephone and her voice shook also. "Not today. I couldn't face anyone new today. I'll be fine. But tell me what happened. Was it an accident? What?"

"They've just started the investigation." She heard someone calling to Brian. "Yeah," he answered. "Be right there. Gotta go, Gram. I'll call you later."

Fonnie stared at the phone and thought about poor Christine. What kind of accident could have happened?

But, she thought, Brian hadn't confirmed that it was an accident. If not, then what was it? Surely there would be something on TV.

Fonnie reached for the remote that lay on the kitchen table. Brian liked to watch the early news on the 19 inch TV he'd installed on the counter, squeezed in between the toaster and the coffee maker. Since Brian had moved into the house, TVs had invaded the premises like ants on bread crumbs. In addition to her old console in the den, he had placed sets in the kitchen, in his bedroom, in her bedroom, in the enclosed sun room, and in what Harrison used to call the library. It was actually an expanded storage area off the dining room filled with books they couldn't bear to part with. Brian explained to her that he used the VCR in there to view his police academy study tapes, and emphasized that they would be of no interest to her. She suspected he might have some other kinds of tapes in there also, but she didn't pry. Christine had gone into the room one day and came out with a flushed face. Fonnie hadn't inquired about it, but suggested that Brian could do his own cleaning in there in the future.

Fonnie flipped through the Early Show, a cooking show, a rerun of *Gilligan's Island,* and some judge pounding for order in the court. She was reminded again why she watched very little daytime TV, and felt frustrated not to find any breaking news segments about poor Christine. She turned the volume down a little, but left it loud enough so that if a news flash was announced, she'd hear it.

She wished now she'd had followed the debate over the new landfill more closely. Could the battle be so bitter that one side or the other would kill an innocent

bystander? And was Christine innocent? She had expressed antagonism to the Myerson Corporation, but
had denied being a member of CATWAG.

Fonnie tried to remember the snatches of arguments
she'd heard on both sides. Groverton was growing and
certainly needed more space to dump its refuse. The
town was trying to attract new industries that in turn
would generate new wastes. The opponents of the
landfill declared that much of this waste would be toxic.
They listed an impressive number of poisons that the
citizens needed to be protected from: arsenic, lead,
mercury, vinyl chloride. Fonnie felt that whatever these
substances were used for, they should *not* be allowed to
filter into the ground water to be consumed by unwary
citizens. The CATWAGs asserted that the Myerson Corporation had a poor safety record in handling these
wastes in other counties.

On the other hand, the city council, the merchants'
association, the county commissioners, the Groverton
Betterment Committee all praised the foolproof design
of the new landfill. They claimed there was no chance
of leakage of any dangerous chemicals, even if such
chemicals existed in industrial waste products. The
more she thought about it, the more Fonnie wondered
which side to believe. But right now, it didn't matter;
she just wanted to know what the newscasters would say
about the body found at the protest site. What was Christine doing there? What connection did she have with
either side? How and when did she die? And if it wasn't
an accident, what did the police suspect? But there was
nothing on TV yet. It may be that the police were with-
holding any information until their investigation got
under way, or until they notified the next of kin.

The phone shrilled. Fonnie snatched it up, hoping it was Brain with more news. It wasn't. "Mrs. Beachum, this is the Family Home Health Service. I'm so sorry that Christine won't be able to visit you this morning. But I can send a replacement within an hour."

The woman's calm voice irritated Fonnie. Was she just going to pretend that Christine was out of work with a slight cold? That she could send a replacement and that the world would be right side up again? Fine. Two could play at that game. "Oh?" Fonnie said. "Is she ill?"

"Not exactly. It seems that Christine has had an accident." The voice faltered and then went bravely on. "But I'm sure you'll be happy with one of our other aides."

Fonnie winced. She hadn't actually been happy with Christine, but the nurse's aide deserved a better goodbye than she was getting. But maybe I'm being too harsh, Fonnie thought. Perhaps the police told the agency not to say anything about Christine's death until they could locate the family. That must be it. "No," Fonnie said. "Don't send anyone else. I'll call you tomorrow about a replacement." Fonnie hung up before the woman could reply. A cloud of sadness dropped down over her like a shroud—sadness that some lives were gone in an instant while others seemed never to quit.

Fonnie made her way over to the computer. Her conversation with Brian seemed so unreal she felt she had to get it down in black and white before she could believe it. She carefully dated her entry as she always did and started typing, paying no attention to punctuation or incomplete sentences.

October 15

Brian just called to tell me that Christine is dead. Her body was found at the new landfill site. Don't know if it was accident or not.

That's when her imagination kicked in and her questions started.

But if it wasn't an accident then what? Murder? Suicide? And why the landfill? What was she doing there? What was she wearing? Her uniform scrubs? Dress clothes? Nothing?

That last word evoked some terrible images and Fonnie didn't even want to suggest them on paper. She shook her head, reread the few lines, marveled at the way the computer automatically put in the capital letters she'd neglected. More questions shoved their way into her brain.

Was her car there? Was she robbed? Brian said they found her ID so they must have her purse or billfold, but what about her money?

"This is stupid," Fonnie said to the screen, to her brain, to the too-quiet house. She clicked the print icon and leaned back while the printer groaned into action. "No use asking more questions now. I'll just have to wait until Brian gets home."

Fonnie needed to talk to someone—someone other than herself. A few of her old friends had called and had come to visit since she'd been home. They'd chatted, talked about how time was getting away, about colleagues who had passed on, about how the weather seemed colder than when they were young. But their conversations had steered away from important items: lonely days, lonelier nights, fears of the future. She couldn't very well call any of them and say her home-health aide had been killed and she was afraid. They'd probably ask what she was afraid of, and she wouldn't have an answer.

She didn't know why a capsule of fear had taken up residence in her gut. Before this happened, she'd begun to feel comfortable being home again, being alone much of the day, but now her carefully built defense system began to crumble.

Maybe Amy would be in her office. It would be good to talk to her daughter. Fonnie kept hoping that their relationship would improve, and that Amy's opposition to Brian's job choice would mellow some. Brian tried to act like it didn't bother him, but Fonnie knew differently.

As she reached for the phone, she recalled trying to make small talk with the aide on her first day of work. Their conversation had a staccato quality.

"Do you have any children?" Fonnie had asked.

"Two boys. Grown. Don't see them much."

"Any grandchildren?"

"Not that I know of."

There was no mention of a husband, past or present, and Fonnie felt uncomfortable asking. Instead she inquired rather fatuously. "Do you enjoy your work?"

"Sure. Why not?"

Another time while Christine was washing dishes, Fonnie had tried to start a conversation by asking, "Am I your only patient?"

"Nope. I do old Mrs. Whitehall in the afternoons."

"Whitehall? Any relation to our county commissioner, Ed Whitehall?"

"His mother."

"Oh. She must be getting on in years."

"Yeah."

Fonnie didn't pursue that line of questioning. Being a nurse, she knew patient information was confidential, so she swerved the talk to the patient's son. "I've admired Ed Whitehall for years, though I've never met him. From what I read about him, he really seems to be committed to the county's welfare. What's he like in person?"

The glass Christine had in her hand slipped out of her fingers and smashed on the floor. Apologies and clean-up occupied the next few minutes. The question never was answered.

Since that day Fonnie had learned little more about Christine—except the fact that she had opposed the landfill. She dialed Amy's number and the thought occurred to her that Amy might have known Christine. They were probably close to the same age. They could have been in school together. Fonnie wasn't sure whether Christine had gone to public school here or what her maiden name was, but she could find out from Brian. Amy's phone rang three times and then the voice mail kicked in and politely asked her to leave a message. Fonnie didn't like speaking to machines. She made it short. "Just wanted to talk, dear. But I'll e-mail you instead." She started to hang up, then brought the phone back to her lips. "Love you."

Amy was never out of communication range for long. In her real estate business she couldn't afford to be, so she regularly picked up her e-mails and voice messages. Before heading back to the computer, Fonnie made a detour to the microwave. Christine had thoughtfully arranged a container of tea bags, a jar of instant coffee, a sugar bowl, and some cups on the counter so Fonnie could easily fix herself a hot drink. Brian had bought an old wheeled teacart at a flea market, cleaned it up, fixed a wobbly wheel and presented it to his grandmother. It was perfect for transporting things from the stove or refrigerator to the table or to her favorite recliner or to the computer. She had merely to aim it in the right direction, and then to push it forward with her cane. This morning, she decided she wanted Mandarin Orchard Green Tea. She fixed the tea, added some shortbread cookies to the tray and headed back to the den.

In between sips, she typed her news to Amy.

Dear Amy,
I called your office but you were out. Didn't want to use your cell phone. I know you're busy. But I feel I must tell you what has happened.

She went on to type what little she knew of Christine's death, but didn't mention her own fears.

Fonnie moved the cart, along with the telephone, over to the recliner, turned the TV on low, propped her feet up and finished her tea. Amy's response came within the hour. Fonnie was glad it was by phone instead of e-mail.

"Mom. Are you all right? What a dreadful thing to happen. I know you must be terribly upset. Has Brian found out anything else?"

Her daughter's concern rattled Fonnie even more. The phone shook as Fonnie tried to control the tremor in her voice. "I am rather upset. Just natural, I guess. Christine was due here at eight this morning and when she didn't show, I became angry with her." Fonnie's voice broke. "And all the time the poor thing was lying out there in the cold, all alone—dead. I feel so bad."

"There, there, Mom, don't fret about it. Try to get your mind on something else."

"I can't. The agency offered to send someone to take Christine's place, but I'm not up to breaking in anyone new."

"You won't have to break anyone in. I'm coming down tonight to spend a day with you. I intended to when you first got home, but things were rather piled up here. Now I have a handle on everything and it'll be all right to leave."

"That's wonderful, dear. It'll be so good to have you around for awhile. It's nice to be home, but the time hangs so heavy on my hands when I'm alone. I can't seem to get interested in reading and I can't do much else."

"We'll find something for you to do. How about cross-stitching? You could do that with one hand. And you used to like to do crossword puzzles. You need a project to keep your mind busy."

After they hung up, Fonnie thought about what Amy had said. She did need something to keep her mind from going mushy. Something to stimulate her brain cells. But what?

She glanced up at the TV screen and was greeted with the flashing words *Breaking News*. She turned up the volume and listened carefully as the announcer's solemn voice explained the scene of protesters, police and curious onlookers. "A body was found this morning at the site of the proposed landfill. The cause of death has not yet been determined. Foul play has not been ruled out. The victim is forty-four-year-old Christine Hauner, an employee of the Family Home Health Agency." Fonnie held her breath, hoping the camera was not going to show poor Christine's body. It didn't. "It's not known what connection, if any, Hauner had with the protesters, but one of them was able to identify the body."

The camera then swung to a policeman who looked startled and said only, "A statement will be forthcoming."

Fonnie searched the crowd on the screen for a sight of Brian. There were several uniformed police persons there, but she couldn't identify Brian among them. She continued to stare at the crowd milling around. She saw Ms. Franklin and Ed Whitehall pushing their way toward a big black car. The thought came to her that by now, Ed would have learned the identity of the victim. His aging mother was Christine's other patient. Was he as upset by Christine's death as she was?

As she contemplated this question, the door opened and Brian swept in. He gave his grandmother a quick peck on the cheek, "Just came home for a bite of lunch." He turned his attention to the TV. "What are they saying?"

"Not much. You policemen are pretty closed-mouthed with reporters."

"Have to be. Can't say anything that might impede the investigation."

"Of course, but I'm not a reporter and I have no intention of impeding any investigation, so feel free."

Brian grinned and rolled his eyes. "Free? Whatever do you mean?"

"Don't get smart with me, young man. You know exactly what I mean. Fill me in. Was Christine's death an accident? What was the cause of death? When did it happen? What was she doing out there? Do you have any suspects?" Fonnie paused for two quick breaths. "And did she suffer?"

Brian became instantly serious. "The chief is giving a news conference this afternoon so I can tell you most of what he's going to say. Keep in mind, I'm only telling you what is going around at the station. I'm not in on the investigation. But I think this is what we know to date. Her death was not an accident. She appeared to have been beaten to death—by someone bigger and stronger—and probably very angry. And it's hard to say if she suffered. The first blow may have killed her—or maybe not."

Fonnie cringed, but said nothing.

"As to when it happened—the time of death was probably last night sometime—perhaps before midnight. And no, they don't have any suspects."

"But what was she doing at the landfill site?"

"She was brought there."

Fonnie gasped. "Brought there? Just thrown out? Like garbage—or toxic waste?"

"Looks like. And the body wasn't hidden. Whoever put her there must have wanted her found this morning."

"So the murder must have something to do with the landfill and the protestors."

"Too early to speculate about that."

But Fonnie was speculating. The strain that had covered her face the last hours began to fade away as her brain started spinning. "A warning. That must be it." She flopped back in the recliner, swiped at her hair. "But to which side?"

Brain shrugged. "I have to get back. I'm just going to make a quick sandwich and get gone."

"Wait a minute. A couple of other things. What was she wearing and were there tire tracks?"

Brian shook his head at his grandmother. "Oh no. Now don't you go thinking I'm going to come home and tell you everything I know. This is police business and it's going to stay that way." He headed toward the kitchen. "Besides," he added, "remember I'm still a rookie. I won't be working homicide."

"Of course. I understand, and I wouldn't dream of asking for confidential information. But you were there this morning and saw the body. Surely you can answer two simple questions." Fonnie put on her pouting face: lower lip extended, chin quivering ever so slightly, eyes lowered. It was a childish gesture, but she figured an old woman should be allowed to use whatever means she had.

"Okay. But from now on you'll have to get your details from the TV like everybody else."

Fonnie nodded in agreement. "Well, she was wearing jeans, a sweatshirt and tennis shoes."

"And tire tracks?"

"Pretty hard to tell. Tracks all over the place where surveyors had been in and out. And then the bulldozers this morning. But the lab boys are working on it." Brian again headed for the kitchen. "Now I really have to eat and run."

"Fine. By the way, your mother is coming down tonight."

"Mom? I'm surprised she can pull herself away from her precious job." Brian slapped his mouth and let out a deep sigh. "I'm sorry. I shouldn't have said that. I respect her profession. I just wish she'd respect mine."

"She will. Give her time." Fonnie smiled. "She may even forgive me some day for siding with you."

"Are you sorry you did?"

"Not at all. If being a cop makes you happy, then that's what you should do." Brian bobbed his head. Fonnie finished her thought in a low whisper, "Even if it could be dangerous."

Brian devoured a ham and Swiss, then slammed out the back door. Fonnie muted the TV and attempted to put her thoughts about Christine in some kind of order. She tried her best to remember anything out of the ordinary in the aide's behavior.

Fonnie recalled the day she'd asked Christine to make some "sun" tea.

"You mean, just let the tea brew in the sun instead of using boiling water?"

"Yes. I have a quart jar I use and I set it in the south kitchen window. Three or four hours of that sunlight and the tea is ready to add ice cubes and sugar. Perfect."

"But you use bottled water, don't you?"

"Of course not. Why should I do that? There's nothing wrong with my tap water." Fonnie remembered being perturbed with her even though Christine had made no further comment and proceeded to follow instructions.

And, Fonnie thought, Christine had been sad. It was in her eyes. She went about her work easily enough, but her eyes had that faraway look as if they were trying to remember how to smile.

IT WAS NEARLY NOON by the time Bebe got back home. No one had wanted to leave the landfill site until they knew what had happened. That part didn't take long. News of a dead body scuttled around the assemblage faster than an e-mail virus. Then one of the policemen decided he needed the name and address of each person there. While this was in progress, crime-scene technicians and more police personnel arrived, followed closely by an ambulance.

Before the ambulance drove out, Sergeant Vic Helms came up to Bebe and asked if she knew Christine Hauner. She shook her head. "I don't think so. The name doesn't ring a bell."

Neil Vincent interrupted. "Sure you know her. She's been to a couple of your meetings. Plump, middle-aged, kind of shy. Remember? I talked to her one night after the meeting. She supported your," here Neil hesitated and his cold-reddened face became even redder, "that is, *our* cause, but couldn't actually become a member of CATWAG because her employer would disapprove."

Bebe gave him a cold stare, "Just like your situation, eh?"

Neil shrugged and turned back to Vic. "Is that who it is?"

"That's what her ID says. How about stepping over here to see if you recognize her."

Neil gulped a deep breath of frosty air. "Well, I didn't really know her. Just saw her a couple of times."

"Good enough. Come on." Vic motioned toward the ambulance. "You should be able to identify her. Her face isn't beat up too much."

Bebe felt a brief moment of sympathy for Neil as she noted the flush leaving his face to be replaced by a sickly pallor.

After the ambulance left, Bebe saw Neil make his way to his car. Vic came over to her again. "You can go now." He gave her a polite smile. "But someone will probably be by later to talk to you."

"Why? I told you I didn't know her."

"Gotta cover all the bases. Bye now. Take care."

"Yeah, sure. You too."

BEBE KICKED OFF her boots, slipped some wooly socks on her frigid feet, and zapped some leftover breakfast coffee in the microwave. She collapsed in the leather recliner just in time for the twelve o'clock news. The news anchor didn't have much more information than she did—only that Christine Hauner worked for the Family Home Health Service. When the announcer stated that foul play could not be ruled out, Bebe nearly choked on her coffee. "What in the hell else could it be?" she demanded of the TV screen. "This gal was taking an early morning stroll and tripped over a rock? Get real."

The next few hours Bebe alternated between trying to figure out what might have happened to Christine and trying to put the whole tragic incident out of her mind. Neither effort was successful.

Late in the afternoon Neil called. "Has the detective been there yet?"

"What detective?"

"Dickson. With homicide. He just left here. Was questioning me about what I knew."

"And what do you know?"

"Nothing. Like I told him. I only spoke to Christine a few minutes after one of your meetings. It was the meeting last month when you were telling people if they really supported the fight for a safe environment, they would become official CATWAG members. A bunch of people signed on the dotted line that night. You know, you would have made a great preacher. You really know how to get people fired up."

"Yeah. Everybody except you and Hauner. What did you say to her?"

"Well, she was just kind of standing around after you finished, like she didn't know what to do. So I went up and asked her if she was going to join. And she said she would like to, but if she did she might lose her job. And I told her I understood, because being a teacher, I have to go along with what the school board thinks."

"That's a bunch of bull." Bebe forced a laugh. She really did like Neil and didn't want to make him mad, but she wished he had more of a backbone. "I recall you didn't have any qualms about marching to get a bigger pay raise. You weren't going along with the school board then."

"That was different."

"Sure. Then you were just a peon. Now you're in line to become principal and you don't want to screw up. Right?"

"Right. And I'm not going to apologize for it. Now do you want me to continue about Christine or not?"

"Yes, please. Sorry I got off track."

"So, after I told her that, she seemed to relax some. She told me she felt she ought to become involved because she lives close to where the landfill would be and she didn't want to be drinking poisoned water. And get this. She said, and I quote, 'It wouldn't surprise me none if Groverton's water was already poisoned.'"

"Wo-o-ow." Bebe had to take a deep breath to make up for all the air she lost on that one long syllable. "Do you think she knew something we don't?"

"I doubt it. I think your sermon just made her a little hysterical."

The ping-ping of Bebe's doorbell interrupted any retort she was about to make. From her recliner, she had a clear view of the front porch and the man standing at the door. "What does this detective look like?"

"Tall, skinny, wears a brown suit, chews on a cigar."

"That must be him at the door. Although he's ditched the cigar. Talk to you later."

Bebe hung up, dropped the phone, and hurried to the door. She put on a pleasant face. "Yes?"

"Mrs. Englehook?"

"Yes. May I help you?"

Lieutenant Dickson was polite, but to the point. After introducing himself and flashing his ID, he showed Bebe a picture of an unsmiling woman with fat cheeks, frizzy hair, and blank eyes staring straight into the camera. "Recognize her?"

Bebe studied the picture. "From her driver's license?"

The detective nodded.

"I don't know how the DMV manages to make everybody look like either a convict or an imbecile. Mine looks like both."

Dickson grinned. "Mine too. But to get back to the case in point. Have you seen her before?"

"Yes. I never actually met her, but I do remember seeing her at a couple of CATWAG meetings. She sat in the back of the room—by herself. Neil Vincent said he had a conversation with her, but I never did."

"So she wasn't among the people you were expecting for the protest march?"

Bebe shook her head. "She hadn't signed up for it.

Of course, anybody was welcome, but I only had enough signs painted for those who had said they would come."

"If you think of anything, anything at all, that might have a bearing on the case, please give me a call." He handed Bebe his business card.

It wasn't until the detective left that Bebe remembered seeing Neil leaning against the fence when she first arrived at the landfill site. Why was he at the site so early? What was he doing by the fence? Did he see anything unusual?

FIVE

FONNIE WAS DELIGHTED when Amy called again to say she'd be there about six, and that she'd bring dinner. Brian called later and said he knew nothing more about the case. He was going out with some buddies and would be home late. Maybe it was just as well, Fonnie thought. She didn't want any family discord to mar Amy's arrival. Mother and son could work on their differences, if they wished, at a later time. Right now Fonnie was glad she would have Amy to herself, and perhaps they could do a little fence-mending of their own.

Fonnie heard the car just as the automatic yard light came on. She turned off the news broadcast. The only new information about Christine's death was that the police were now calling it a homicide.

A brief interview with Ms. Scoggins of the Family Home Health Services followed. "Christine Hauner had worked for us over three years," Ms. Scoggins said. "She was a loyal and well-loved employee. She will be greatly missed." When the reporter asked Ms. Scoggins if she had any comment about the death being a homicide, she replied, "I knew very little about her personal life. I only know she was a good employee."

As Fonnie hurried to the back door, she agreed with what Ms. Scoggins had implied, that Christine's death had nothing to do with her employment.

She opened the door to a gust of crisp autumn air and Amy's warm hug. She returned the embrace as best she could while maintaining her balance on the quad cane. "Come in this house, youngun'. You're letting in the Arctic air."

"Hardly Arctic. Just invigorating."

"It may be invigorating to you. To me, it's downright cold."

"All right. Let me set my bag down and run back to the car for our dinner. I stopped at Barker's Buffet and loaded up on all your favorites. We're going to feast tonight."

Fonnie held the door open when Amy returned with a plastic bag full of Styrofoam containers. The aromas radiating from the bag made Fonnie's gastric juices start flowing. "I declare," she said, "smells like an old-fashioned Sunday dinner—the kind I used to make a hundred years ago."

Amy started unloading the containers on the kitchen table. "And the kind you'll be making again one day soon. Barker's food is good, but their mashed potatoes and green bean casserole can't compare with yours. Nor their carrot cake."

"You got carrot cake?" Fonnie hurried to the table as fast as she could, collapsed in a chair, and spread her hands heavenward. "The gods be praised! A beautiful daughter and carrot cake. What more could a doddering old woman ask for?"

Amy's lips started to grin and then plunged into a pout. "Enjoy it while you can. And don't worry about leaving any for Brian. He called me and said he had plans for tonight. I think he's avoiding me. He's not ready yet to discuss his career choice with me."

Fonnie watched her daughter as she reached for plates

and glasses to set the table. Amy was beautiful, but frown lines were beginning to etch down the sides of her mouth and a deep furrow often appeared between her pretty jade-green eyes. What had happened to her happy, comical, adventuresome daughter? Was she never going to recover from being abandoned by a scoundrel husband and the responsibility of rearing a son alone?

Fonnie jerked her mind back to what Amy had been saying. "And are you?"

"Am I what?" Amy sounded startled.

"Are you ready to discuss his career choice with him? That is, are you ready to listen to him? Really listen?"

Amy pulled out a chair and sat down. Her hands trembled slightly as she passed the slaw to Fonnie. "I have listened, Mom. And I do understand. It's about his need for fulfillment, to be doing something worthwhile." Her fork played with the strands of cabbage on her plate, then looked up with moistened eyes. "But what about my need? I need to know that the boy I raised isn't putting himself in danger every day. That he isn't going to end up maimed—or dead." Amy reached over, squeezed her mother's hand, gave her a rueful smile. "I need to know he'll be around when I'm a doddering old woman like you."

A gust of wind rattled the wind chime on the back porch. Its frantic tinkling filled the silence between the two women. Fonnie nodded. "I understand. I wish I didn't, but I do."

"What's that supposed to mean?"

"It means that I can see both sides of the situation. That ability has been the bane of my life. Whenever I try to get worked up for some crusade, no matter how noble it is, my mind jerks me around and says, 'but what about the other side of the story?' It makes it very difficult to expound alleged injustices or to march for equal rights or to wave a banner demanding attention for any *cause celebre*."

Amy laughed. "Like the time when I was in high school and the students were demonstrating for the right to leave the school grounds during lunch hour? You championed both sides until my friends and I were so confused we just gave up the fight."

"That's right. Like this landfill fight now. Groverton definitely needs a new landfill and the Myerson Corporation submitted the low bid and had all the necessary studies done. It seems simple enough. But, then along comes the opposition and says Myerson has a poor safety record and we are in danger of them contaminating the ground water and other problems. And I can see both sides of the case—or at least I want to see both sides. Actually I need more information."

Fonnie scooped more potatoes and gravy onto her plate and added another piece of broiled chicken breast. "But I shouldn't be talking about landfills and garbage when I'm eating foods fit for the gods."

"You're right," Amy said, "and I certainly don't want to talk about poor Christine until we're finished."

After a few minutes, Fonnie pushed back her empty plate and reached for the carrot cake. Amy waited while her mother took a big bite, licked a stray bit of cream cheese icing off her lips, and gave a groan of delight. "Now that you're in a receptive mood," Amy said, "I have a pleasant surprise for you."

"Oh? I love surprises. Did you bring me something else?"

"Only some good news. I've hired another aide to

work with you a few hours a day. She can only work until the end of the year, but by that time you should be pretty well independent again."

Fonnie laid down her fork and shook her head. "I'm not sure I can handle having another home health aide coming into my home. I would constantly be thinking of what happened to Christine, and that I should have made an effort to know her better. And, besides, it's so much trouble to orient someone new to my needs and quirky wants."

"What happened to Christine had nothing to do with you. And the person I've hired already knows all about your quirks, your sometimes caustic wit, and loves you anyway."

"My caustic wit? The closest I come to being caustic these days is when I burn my oatmeal. When it comes to dealing with people, I'm the poster girl for propriety. I've learned that when you're dependent on somebody to wash your back, you better not give her an excuse to put a knife into it."

"Bravo. And it only took you seventy some years to learn that. There might be hope for you yet."

Fonnie sipped her iced tea sweetened with enough sugar to make all the disciples of artificial sweeteners shudder. "So—who is this person who knows my quirks and wit and supposedly loves me anyway?"

"Keisha Riggs. Remember her?"

"Keisha? Bold, black, beautiful Keisha from Spring-willow?" Fonnie's lips curved into a new-moonlike bow, deepening her wrinkles, but lighting up her eyes. "She left there to go to college. How did you get hold of her?"

"It's called connections. I knew she'd enrolled in Groverton Community College and I happen to have a friend who has a sister on the faculty there and, to make a long story short, I got her phone number and called her." Amy's smile was nearly as wide as Fonnie's. "I remembered how fond you were of her and so I took a chance that she might have some time she could spare for you. And she does. Her classes are in the afternoon, so she has agreed to come for two or three hours in the mornings. There's no agency involved. It's strictly a private arrangement and I'm going to pay her."

Fonnie felt her eyes filling with grateful tears. She groped for a tissue, sniffed and dabbed before she was able to say anything, and then all she could manage was a simple, "Thank you."

Amy nodded. "Sure. She's coming over in the morning to work out a schedule with you. She can start on Wednesday."

"That's great. It'll be so good to see her again."

"And, Mom, I have some other news for you too."

"Couldn't be any better than what you've already told me."

A soft blush suffused Amy's cheeks. "Depends on your point of view."

"Sounds special. Tell me."

"I'm dating a very nice gentleman. His name is Paul Trent. He's an attorney, a widower, an Episcopalian, and has one married daughter—no grandkids yet."

"And you're crazy about him."

Amy laughed. "You don't tiptoe around, do you? But you're almost right. I'm very fond of him—and he of me, but we're not crazy kids. He's a very nice gentleman, and we just enjoy each other's company."

"Of course. I'm glad for you." Fonnie took a last bite of cake and winked at her daughter. "You know, I wouldn't mind having a very nice gentleman of my own around. Does he, perhaps, have an older brother?" Fonnie enjoyed watching the flow of emotions on Amy's face: embarrassment, pretended shock, and finally playfulness.

"Not an older brother. I might be able to scrounge up an eccentric uncle. Paul mentioned one who collects ping-pong balls and has a pet armadillo. I think you two might hit it off."

"Sounds good. When we get tired of tossing ping-pong balls, we can race the armadillo. But maybe I ought to meet Paul first to see if I approve of the family before getting involved with his uncle."

"Right, but I don't know when that will be. He stays pretty busy. I'll bring him down some weekend." Amy took a quick swallow of tea. "I know you'll like him, Mom. I just wonder if Brian will."

THE EVENING NEWS repeated all that was known about Christine Hauner's death, along with information about the landfill controversy. The news commentator linked the two events together. Not only because Christine's body was found at the site, but because she was identified as a sympathizer of the protest group.

When a snapshot of Christine was shown, Amy shook her head. "How terrible. To die in a garbage dump. She looks about my age, but I don't recognize her. But then, I guess I wouldn't. They said she was originally from Virginia and moved here about three years ago. I wonder what brought her here. Did she say anything to you about it?"

"No. And I didn't ask. She didn't seem to want to talk about her personal life. She said she had two sons, but

I got the impression that they didn't live around here. All I really know is that she worked in the afternoons caring for Ed Whitehall's mother."

"Ed Whitehall? Wasn't his name just mentioned as a county commissioner?"

"Yep. He's one of the main backers of the Myerson Corporation. He and Dale seem to be really buddy-buddy. I've seen them on news segments before. That is, before poor Christine was found. Whitehall was adamant about Myerson's integrity. Said his safety record was unassailable."

"I don't understand what's behind all the protests. These CATWAG people must have something to go on." Amy turned the volume down on the TV when the reporter mentioned another break-in of an empty house. Fonnie's thoughts turned to the break-in of her own house before she had come home and wondered if there might be a connection. But her attention was diverted when Amy asked, "And who is this Dale you mentioned?"

"Dale Myerson, the president of Myerson Corporation. Can you believe that he and I went to high school together?"

"No way! If he's that old, how come he's still working?"

"What do you mean 'that old' and why shouldn't he still be working?"

"Okay, Mom, don't get your tail in a knot." Amy covered her mouth to stifle a giggle. "You know what I mean. He has to be past retirement age."

"He is, but not by much. He's a few years younger than I am, but I remember him well. He had that certain aura of success even then."

Fonnie rubbed her right hand across her chin and felt

a rough stubble. Darn, she thought, Christine didn't shave me last week. The thinner my hair gets on top, the more chin whiskers I sprout. Another humiliating aspect of growing old.

She jerked her mind back to Dale Myerson, a little envious that he had retained much of his youthful handsomeness along with a full head of hair. She smiled as an idea danced into her head. "You know what I'm going to do?"

"I never know what you're going to do so I'll skip the guessing. Just come out with it."

"I'm going to invite Dale over here—for lunch or maybe even dinner. We can renew our acquaintance, talk about old Prescott High, and I can get the facts about the landfill."

"Sounds good. Just a few problems."

"And they would be?"

"He may not remember you. He may not want to come. If he does come, who's going to do the cooking? And lastly, you'll only get the facts he wants you to hear."

"Oh, he'll remember me. Your uncle Morris was his campaign manager when Dale ran for president of his class. He'll come because people from small towns, and Prescott is even smaller than Groverton, are polite and they don't refuse invitations from old friends. And no one will cook because I'll order from Barker's just like you did. And I know he'll only tell me his side of the story. But that's okay." Fonnie gave her chin stubble one more stroke and came up with the second part of her plan. "Because the next day I'll invite the president of CATWAG over to tell me the other side."

After dinner Fonnie stretched out in the recliner and struggled to keep her eyes open during *Wheel of Fortune*.

Amy curled up in a corner armchair with her cell phone. "I'm going to check my messages and then give Paul a ring. I told him I'd call tonight."

"By all means," Fonnie murmured. "Don't let that very nice gentleman forget you while you're gone."

Amy smiled. "And should I inquire about his uncle and the armadillo?"

"Not tonight. I don't want to appear too eager."

By the time Amy finished her phone calls, Fonnie was nearly asleep. "Come on, Mom. I'd better tuck you in bed. You've had a hard day." Amy helped her out of the chair, to the bathroom, and into her flannel nightgown.

As Fonnie's head sank into her pillow, she heard Brian come whistling into the house. "There's our boy now," she said. "Tell him goodnight for me, dear."

"Will do. Rest well." Amy bent over, kissed her mother lightly on the cheek. "Love you."

Fonnie wondered briefly what kind of conversation Amy and Brian would have, but she was too sleepy to wonder for long.

FONNIE AWOKE to the scent of cinnamon rolls, the aroma of hazelnut coffee, and the sweet sound of her daughter humming. It had been such a long time since Amy had actually seemed happy that Fonnie said a little prayer of thanks for Paul Trent. She just hoped he was as nice as Amy had presented him.

When she heard Brian clumping down the stairs, Fonnie decided she'd better bestir herself. She had pretty well perfected the out-of-bed, to-the-bathroom, getting-her-robe-on routine. The teeth and hair brushing still needed some improvement. It was difficult for her to balance while using her one good hand to hold the brushes. She managed by propping her left side against the sink and grasping the toilet paper holder with her still weak left hand. She had gotten a new perm and hair rinse before leaving the nursing home, so her curls were still perky and coppery red. She knew the color was ridiculous, but it had suited her defiant mood at the time. Maybe she had to accept the limitations of her body, but she could control the color of her hair.

Brian was wiping his lips when Fonnie entered the kitchen. "Morning, Gram. I had forgotten what a mean omelet Mom could make. You'd better try one."

"That's right. Get your order in while the cook is still on duty." Amy waved the spatula in her right hand and sipped from the cup of coffee in her left. "It isn't often I get in the domestic mode. Of course, the cinnamon rolls were prepackaged, but everything else is made from scratch."

Brian untangled his long legs from his chair, stood up, patted his stomach. "Now that's a meal a man can go to work on. And that's where I've got to go right now."

Fonnie beamed as Brian walked over and pecked his mother's cheek. "You know, Gram," he said, turning to Fonnie, "I think Mom's new boyfriend is having a good effect on her."

"So she told you and you approve?"

"Sure. She'll have something to think about instead of worrying about me."

Amy quickly turned her back. Her hand shook slightly as she poured more coffee and her voice trembled. "I'll never stop worrying about you."

Brian shrugged his shoulders. "Well, anyway, I've got to go. See you tonight?"

"I don't think so. I need to be getting back." She

walked over, wrapped her arms around the gangly boy in the police uniform. "Take care of yourself."

Brian brushed his mother's hair with his lips. Fonnie couldn't hear what he murmured, but Amy nodded and turned back to the stove.

As sweet as the scene was, it jerked Fonnie's mind back to the horrible event that had brought Amy here in the first place. She called Brian back as he was scooting out the kitchen door. "Don't you dare leave until you tell me the latest about the investigation. What have they found out about Christine's past? Where was she killed? Why was she killed?"

Brian stopped in mid-stride. "I don't know anything more. And chances are I won't know anything. Remember I'm just a rookie, not a homicide detective. You'll have to get your news the way everybody else does—the newspaper and TV."

"But if you do happen to overhear anything, you'll tell me. Right?"

"Right. Now I've really gotta go."

Fonnie waved her cane in a goodbye salute, then another thought came to her. "Wait!" Brian waited, a resigned smile on his face. "Can you at least tell me who is the lead detective on the case?" Fonnie asked.

"Sure. It's Lieutenant Mike Dickson. Nice guy."

A plan began to form in Fonnie's mind as she waved goodbye to Brian. "So get gone already." Fonnie sipped her coffee and plotted her day. She looked up at Amy. "What time did you say Keisha was coming?"

"About ten."

"Good. Then there's time for a couple of phone calls."

"Are you really going to call Dale Myerson?"

"No. You're going to do that."

"Me? Why me?"

"Because you have a more authoritarian phone voice than I do. I don't know where he's staying or how long he's going to be in town. But you can find out for me."

Amy dropped in the chair opposite her mother and poured herself some orange juice. "And how can I do that?"

"There are only two decent motels in town. He and his entourage must be staying at one of them. You call and ask. And when they connect you to some underling, you explain that you have an urgent message from an old friend and that the old friend will talk to no one except the boss himself. Then when he comes on the phone, hand it to me and I'll reintroduce myself."

"Sounds simple. But what if he refuses to talk to me?"

"Then say something to the effect that perhaps the newspapers would be interested in the message."

Amy nearly choked on her last swallow of juice. "Mom, that's terrible. How will you explain it when you do finally talk to him?"

"Let me worry about that. Actually, as far as I know, Dale is a perfectly upstanding and honest man and always has been. But it isn't difficult to cast doubt on anybody that's in the news. I'll just tell him it was a little joke to get his attention."

"All I can say is that you better serve him a mighty good lunch when he gets here." Amy reached for the telephone book and her cell phone.

The process was much simpler than either Fonnie or Amy had anticipated, and no threats were necessary. When Fonnie explained she was Morris Wyandotte's big sister and that she wanted to renew their acquaintance and implied she was impressed by his business acumen, Dale accepted her invitation quickly. The luncheon date was made for one the next afternoon.

After she hung up, Fonnie immediately dialed another number. Amy looked surprised. "Whom are you calling now?"

"The police station."

"You can't bother Brian at work."

"It's not Brian I'm calling." She counted the rings until a pleasant voice answered and Fonnie announced her business. "Detective Dickson, please."

"He's not in at the moment. May I ask who's calling?"

"Fonnie Beachum. Please ask him to call me as soon as he has a chance. Tell him I have information regarding Christine Hauner's murder." Fonnie heard Amy gasp, but didn't look in her direction.

"Oh. Well, just hang on a moment. He may have just come in."

Again, getting what she wanted was amazingly simple. Lieutenant Dickson agreed to come by her house that afternoon.

Amy busied herself carrying dirty dishes to the sink and tried to keep her voice calm. "You can't go around telling lies to the police. You don't know anything about Christine's murder. What will Brian think?"

"Brian doesn't have to know about it. And I don't tell lies—very often. Besides, all I said was that I had some information—and I do. I can tell the detective how sad Christine seemed and what she said about my water."

"What's wrong with your water?"

"Nothing. That is, I don't think there is, but Christine apparently thought so. That's information the police need to know. It may lead to something else. And, of course, while I'm telling him what I know, he may well tell me what he knows. So we both win."

"Mom, you're impossible."

Fonnie finished her breakfast and went to her room. She struggled into her bright green sweat suit, rubbed a little natural pine scented oil on her wrists, and applied a smidgen of Raspberry Whisper lipstick. Then she went to the den to await Keisha's arrival. When the doorbell rang, Fonnie motioned Amy back and scrambled to the door.

Fonnie was so glad to see the smiling face under the mat of black kinky hair, that she wanted to give her a hug. In the nursing home they had made a game of teasing each other about their hair; their laughter and hugs coming easily and naturally. But would that be appropriate now? The young lady in front of her was dressed in a smart navy-blue pant suit. She carried a slim purse, and she looked every bit like a prim business person.

As Fonnie hesitated, Keisha broke the ice. "I declare, you look prettier than a Christmas tree—green suit and red hair." She stepped forward, hugged Fonnie around the neck and took a deep sniff. "You even smell like one. And I thought I was going to find an old woman curled up in bed needing my angel-of-mercy hands."

"Come in this house. All this old woman needs is your smiling face." Keisha shut the door and Fonnie led the way down the hall into the den.

Amy came over with outstretched hands. "So good to see you again, Keisha. I'll leave you two to plan your schedule while I finish up the dishes."

Fonnie sat on the sofa and patted the cushion next to her. "Now sit down here and explain yourself."

"Explain myself?"

"Yes. What's the idea of coming here dressed up like a junior executive? I thought college students dressed like they were going to work on a farm."

Keisha laughed. "This old thing? You should see me when I really dress up." She brushed a hair off the sleeve of her jacket. "But to tell the truth I do usually wear jeans and tee shirts and that's what I'll wear here. No more uniforms for me. Okay?"

"Sure. Okay. Frankly, I don't want to see any more uniforms. And I'm flattered you put on your church clothes for me today."

"Don't be. I didn't dress for you. I have an appointment after class today with Tyrone's school counselor and I thought I'd better look decent."

"Tyrone? Oh, your little brother. I remember you mentioning him and that your mother died a few years ago."

"Well, he's my younger brother—sixteen now, but he certainly isn't little. He's taller and bigger and smarter than I am—and more talented. That's what his counselor wants to talk about. She wants him to concentrate more on his art and aim for a scholarship."

"You must be very proud of him. But shouldn't the counselor be talking to your dad rather than you?"

Fonnie noticed Keisha's hands clenching in her lap and she answered in a low, controlled voice. "Dad doesn't think being an artist is a real profession. He wants Tyrone to follow him into the ministry. It's become quite a point of contention between them." Keisha pulled on her hair, then continued. "Dad's not too happy with me either, now that I'm siding with Tyrone."

"I understand," Fonnie said. "Family relationships are tricky. Sometimes people get hurt without anyone intending it."

"Ain't it the truth." Keisha gave a half-smile and pulled a pocket calendar from her purse. "But to the business at hand. I can come from about nine to twelve in the mornings. That will give me time to scoot home and have a quick lunch before going to class. That sound good to you?"

"Sounds perfect. But you can eat lunch here if you wish."

"Thanks, but I'd better check in on Dad. Some days he forgets to eat if I'm not there to remind him."

Amy came into the room pushing the tea cart with three coffee mugs. "This cart is great, Mom. You could even use it to carry dirty dishes to the sink, dirty clothes to the washer, dust cloths and furniture polish. All sorts of things."

"Just a doggone minute. Brian bought that cart so I could carry my coffee or tea to the recliner. That's all I'm going to use it for. You don't need to be thinking up chores for me to do."

Keisha grabbed a mug and took a swallow of the hot, black coffee. Fonnie could tell she was trying not to laugh, but didn't quite succeed. "That's right. Fonnie has me now and I'm very good at thinking up chores."

Fonnie sputtered. "That's not what I meant."

While they drank their coffee, Amy told Keisha of the distinguished company coming the next day, and the lunch that was to be delivered.

"So my first day with you, Fonnie, and you have a date with an old boyfriend." Keisha turned to Amy. "Are you sure it's all right to leave them alone, with no chaperone?"

"Don't you worry about me," Fonnie said. "I can handle any man that comes my way. Amy is planning on fixing me up with an armadillo-loving, ping-pong player."

Keisha laughed. "And on that note, I've got to be going. I'll see you in the morning. Oh, incidentally," she said, as she rose to leave, "I noticed when I came up that your yard is a real mess. You need someone to rake leaves and pick up broken branches."

"I know," Fonnie said, "but Brian doesn't have time, and the neighbor boys I used to depend on have moved way."

"How about if I ask Tyrone? He's always looking for odd jobs. He might be able to come over after school tomorrow."

"That would be good," Amy said. "He can keep track of his hours and I'll send him a check along with yours."

Fonnie shook her head. "No. I'll pay him myself. I know young kids want cash on the barrelhead when they work. None of this waiting for a check in the mail. Keisha, just tell him to come whenever he can and I'll pay him whatever the going rate is."

"Good. I'm sure he'll be glad to do it. I'll let you know tomorrow."

SIX

TUESDAY MORNING Bebe opened the Second Chance Book Store at her regular time of ten. She usually spent the first hour of the day there going over receipts from the previous day, restacking books that customers had pulled out, and planning which books or authors to place in the windows. Since Saturday was usually her busiest day, and since she hadn't opened Monday, she spent quite a bit of time on the account book.

Then with Halloween fast approaching, she decided to redo the window with books that fit the season. It was no problem to find covers featuring witches, ghosts, and vampires.

In the back of her mind she kept thinking that some day there might be a book titled *The Mysterious Death of Christine* or perhaps *The Body at the Landfill*. She was picturing the gruesome cover of a young girl covered with trash when the telephone rang.

"Good morning. Second Chance Book Store. Bebe here."

"Hi, Bebe. This is Neil. Heard anything else?"

"About the murder?"

"Of course, about the murder. Do you think I'm calling about the stock market?"

"You don't have to get testy with me. And why aren't you at school?"

"I am at school. I'm on early lunch this semester. So have you heard anything?"

"Only what was on the news. Do you think I have an inside line to the police department?"

"Now who's being testy?"

"I'm sorry, Neil. Let's start over again. Hope you're feeling well on this lovely fall day. I know you're just as concerned about the investigation as I am. I keep thinking about that poor woman and wondering if maybe she had some damaging information about the Myerson Corporation."

"Yeah, me too. It's weird. You just wanted to have a peaceful demonstration and it turns into a murder. Are you planning on calling off your dogs now?"

Bebe was so caught off guard by Neil's crude comment, it was several seconds before her brain could formulate a response. "If you mean, do I plan to stop opposing Myerson, the answer is no. I'm waiting to hear from the Environmental Defense League about what they plan to do. I doubt if Myerson can do any bull-dozing until the police finish with the crime scene and by that time the courts may step in to stop them."

"But don't you think you ought to call off this Defense League until we know why the Hauner woman was killed? You may be putting yourself in danger."

"Me? In danger?" That thought had never crossed her mind, but maybe Neil had a point. Was Christine Hauner killed as a warning to the opposition? If so, am I not only putting myself in danger, but others with me? Was Neil in danger? The other CATWAG members? The idea made her head swim, her legs rubbery. She groped for her desk chair and slid down in it until her head rested on the back.

She heard a voice in the distance and realized she had dropped the phone on the desk. She picked it up as Neil's voice trembled over the line. "Bebe. Are you there? Are you all right? Talk to me."

"Yes, I'm all right. I'm sorry. I guess I lost it for a minute. I just never really connected the murder to us, I mean, to CATWAG and the demonstration. It's a scary thought."

"I know. I didn't mean to upset you. Listen, I've got to go, but I could come over after school. Maybe I could bring a bottle of wine, and we could talk. And if you don't want to discuss the murder, we'll talk about the weather or football or what books we've read lately. Deal?"

"Not tonight. I need some down time. You understand, don't you?"

"Sure. I understand. Don't worry about it."

Bebe could hear the disappointment in his voice. Maybe, she thought, I do need a diversion. "But we could make it tomorrow if you like. I'll close the store about four. Give me a few minutes and then come on over. You bring the wine and I'll scrounge up some cheese and crackers."

AMY LEFT FONNIE'S HOUSE right after lunch on Tuesday. "I don't want to be around when that detective comes," she told her mother. "You two can have a nice chat about murder and motives and suspects, but I want no part of it. And if you had any sense, you'd stay out of it too. You're just too nosy for your own good."

"I prefer to say I have an inquisitive nature."

"And that inquisitive nature nearly got you killed at the nursing home."

"You exaggerate. Besides, I can hardly get in any

trouble in my own home." Fonnie smiled at her concerned daughter. "I know you worry about me, dear, but there's no need. You run along now. I'll be just fine."

Fonnie pulled the den drapes wide open, drew up the Venetian blinds, and plopped herself on the sofa. She wanted to be able to see Lieutenant Dickson when he approached the front door. When he did, she wasted no time going to open it.

He tipped his head forward in what she assumed was a symbolic gesture of tipping his hat, if he had been wearing a hat. "Mrs. Beachum? I'm Lieutenant Dickson. You said you had some pertinent information for me."

"Yes. So nice to meet you. Come in. I have fresh coffee." She led him around so he could sit in the wing-back chair, and she returned to the sofa. Her trusty tea cart was by her right side. Amy had put the coffee in a thermos pitcher to keep it hot and Fonnie now proceeded to pour two cups. "You look like you could use some."

"You're right about that. It's a little chilly outside." He brushed back his brown hair that matched his brown suit and both blended well with his light blue shirt.

"It was nice of you to call. However, I believe you fibbed a little when you stated you were handicapped and couldn't come down to the station. Looks to me you're able to get around quite well."

Fonnie thought she detected amusement in the detective's voice even though his face was stern. "Yes, well you see, I had a stroke and I am making good progress, but I'm not getting out much, and," she paused and then finished in a flurry, "I can't drive, so I had no way to get there."

"You could have asked your grandson to bring you down."

Fonnie gaped at her caller in surprise. "You know Brian?"

"I've run into him a time or two. He's going to make a fine officer."

"But how did you know he was my grandson? I didn't mention him."

"I did some checking on you after you called." The detective smiled. "All part of the job. I think it's grand you're making such a fine recovery."

"Yes. Grand. Been home two weeks and my aide's been murdered. Not exactly what I expected my home-coming to be."

"I understand how upset you must be. You must have been very fond of her."

"No. I wasn't fond of her. In fact, I really didn't like her much at all. She was tardy most of the time, not par-ticularly hard working, and not very pleasant company." Fonnie took her time stirring sugar into her coffee before continuing. She was surprised at the tears that formed behind her bifocals. "But I feel terrible about her death. Somehow, I feel that it's my fault."

"Your fault? How do you mean?" The detective dug a small brown notebook and a ballpoint pen out of his jacket pocket. "You said you had some information. Just what is it you know about this affair?"

Fonnie thought a minute before answering. "Well," she said, "I don't actually *know* anything. I didn't mean to get you over here on false pretenses. It's just that…."

"Don't worry about that. I was planning on seeing you anyway."

"You were?"

"Of course. We have to talk to everyone who had recent dealings with Mrs. Hauner. You never know what leads we might pick up." Lieutenant Dickson set his coffee cup down and poised his pen over the notebook. "Now then, tell me everything about the deceased that you can. I'll be the one to decide if the information is relevant or not."

So Fonnie began, telling him of Christine's often sad and distracted demeanor, her belligerent reaction to Dale Myerson's TV appearance, her concern over Fonnie's tap water.

Fonnie had a sudden thought. "Do you think I ought to get my water tested for purity?"

"You're on city water, aren't you?"

"Yes."

"Then there's no problem. It's only people who live out of town, who have their own wells, who have to worry about contamination." Lieutenant Dickson looked up from his notebook, chewed on the end of his pen. "Like Christine Hauner, for instance."

"Christine lived out of town and had well water?"

The detective nodded his head. "Sure did. And until just now I hadn't thought about having her water tested, but thanks to you," he said, giving Fonnie a grin, "we'll be doing that."

"Then you do think her death is connected with the landfill controversy?"

"Too early to tell."

"You searched her house?"

"Of course."

"Of course," Fonnie said, her head bobbing over her coffee and her eyes fixed on Lieutenant Dickson. "You would have done that. Was that where she was killed?"

"What makes you ask that?"

"Well, she wasn't killed where she was found, so it

had to be elsewhere. And the first elsewhere I can think of is her house."

"And how do you know she wasn't killed where she was found?" The detective's voice turned frosty, and he jiggled the notebook in his right hand.

"It must have been on the news." Fonnie felt a tinge of uneasiness. Had Brian leaked some information he shouldn't have? If so, she didn't want to get him into any trouble. "Wasn't it on the news broadcast last night?"

Lieutenant Dickson shrugged. "It shouldn't have been. But who knows? A reporter may have overheard some comments not meant for the public."

Fonnie took a deep breath in relief. "That must have been what happened. But you didn't answer my question. Was she killed at her home?"

"Let's just say we're still investigating that."

"I take that for a 'yes,' Lieutenant. May I call you Mike?"

The detective raised his eyebrows, then quickly relaxed them. "Of course. Now could you be more specific about her being sad and distracted? Anything she actually said or did?"

Fonnie sipped her coffee, tapped the fingers of her right hand, studied the man in front of her. His eyes were intelligent, his manner courteous, his smile cautious. She liked him. She'd tell him everything she knew and suspected, and maybe this case could be speedily solved. "Christine didn't want to talk about her private life. Now that's unusual for a woman. Most of us like to talk about ourselves, brag about our kids, drag up old memories, tell of fun activities we did over the weekend, or talk about some TV show we especially liked. Christine did none of these."

"Maybe she was just shy. Or being professional. After all, she was an employee, you were the boss."

"That could have been the explanation at first, but I tried to be friendly to her, let her know that I wanted to talk, that it was all right for her to talk to me. After all, I'm here by myself most of the day, so when she was here I wanted some social interaction, a little pleasant conversation. But it didn't happen. When I asked about her family, she said she had two sons and didn't know if she had any grandchildren. Can you imagine that? Didn't know? What kind of relationship did she have with her boys, anyway?"

Fonnie paused to let Mike know she expected, if not an answer to her question, at least some kind of comment. The detective just shrugged.

"You must have talked to her sons." Again Fonnie paused, but Mike only gave a slight nod of his head. "Well?" she asked.

Mike Dickson smiled. "Well, what?"

"Well, what about them? Do they live here in Groverton? Are they married, have kids? Did they get along with their mother? Are they torn up about her death?"

The detective rubbed his fingers across his lips and waved his notebook in front of Fonnie's face. "I thought I came here to get information—not to give it."

"Come on," Fonnie said, "humor me. If you fill me in on her background, it might jog my memory about what else she may have said."

"Your memory doesn't need jogging." Mike shook his head. "You're just being blatantly nosy. But I guess I can't blame you. So, I'll tell you what I know about her family—can't hurt anything.

"They lived in the southern part of Virginia. Accord-

ing to the sons, their parents' marriage wasn't good—
arguments, fights. She may have been a victim of
spousal abuse, although the older boy insisted it didn't
happen. Keep in mind that I didn't interview them
directly. The sheriff there did that for me." The detective poured himself some more coffee before going on.
"As soon as the youngest boy graduated from high
school, Mrs. Hauner left her husband, came here and
lived with a sister. The sister died a couple of years ago
and left her house to Christine. She apparently wanted
to keep in touch with her sons, but they sided with their
dad and cut off the relationship. Her former husband re-
married, but neither of the boys are married—and no,
she didn't have any grandchildren."

"But how did you find the sons? Their addresses?"

"She had made them beneficiaries of a small life insurance policy."

"How sad. Not just her death, but her life. No wonder
she seemed so melancholy."

"Yes, but it really doesn't have any bearing on her
death. The ex-husband and both boys have alibis. Not
that they were really considered suspects. But getting
back to you. Now that your curiosity is satisfied, let me
hear what else you may know about her."

"I'm afraid not much. I asked her one day about her
other client, Mrs. Whitehall, and it seemed to upset her."

"Upset her? How?"

"I remember I was sitting at the kitchen table while
she was washing the dishes. I merely said that I admired
Ed Whitehall and asked what she thought about him.
And she dropped and broke the glass she was holding."

"Deliberately?"

"I never thought about it at the time, but, maybe it

was deliberate so she wouldn't have to answer the question." Fonnie studied her coffee cup and absent-mindedly stirred in another teaspoon of sugar. "Have you interviewed Mrs. Whitehall yet?"

"I've seen her, but there's no interviewing her. Her mind is long gone. She just lies in bed and stares at the pictures on the wall and the figurines on her dresser. I know Ed, of course, just like I know most of the city and county officials. Fine fellow. Kind of quiet. He said he was satisfied with Christine's work. That he never talked with her much since he was at work when she was at his house."

"And his work is what?"

"Travel agency, business consultant, real estate. He's out of town a lot, but always manages to keep in touch with whatever is going on locally."

"And his wife?"

Mike shook his head. "Died a few years ago. Had one daughter, divorced, died last year. Has one grandson."

"Grandson lives with him?"

Mike laughed. "There you go again. Squirming information out of me, instead of the other way around. I'd better get out of here before I spill everything to you."

"Oh? You have other information then?"

"Wouldn't you like to know?" He crammed his notebook into his jacket pocket and turned toward the door.

"Just one more question," Fonnie said, "and I promise I won't try to pry anything else out of you." In the back of her mind, Fonnie was already forming her line of attack for Brian. But first she had to get all she could from Mike.

"And that would be?" the detective asked.

"Who looked after old Mrs. Whitehall when Christine wasn't there?"

Mike frowned. "Guess there's no reason why I can't answer that. There's a live-in housekeeper, name is Eunice Pruitt. She liked Christine, but they didn't talk much. Now I really have to go."

Fonnie shoved aside the tea cart, pushed herself up with her cane, and held out her right hand. "Thank you for coming. Thank you for listening. And if I think of anything else, I'll give you a call."

"Please do."

FONNIE HAD an uneasy feeling after Lieutenant Dickson left. Had she told him everything about Christine that could be pertinent to the case? Had he taken her information seriously?

As often happened, she felt the need to get her thoughts down on paper, and she hurried over to the computer.

October 16

Was it only yesterday Christine was killed? There couldn't possibly be any progress in the case already. Why was I bugging Mike? I like him. I'm sure he'll follow every clue, every bit of evidence, and will unmask the murderer. So there's nothing I can do. Or is there? Maybe I could talk to others who knew Christine, get more of a sense of who she was, what made her tick. And how am I going to do that? I have no idea—but it will come to me. There's got to be a way to get information—information that will help solve the case. And I've got to try. I owe it to Christine.

SEVEN

BRIAN HAD NOTHING NEW to tell his grandmother that evening about the case, and Fonnie had no intention of telling Brian about Mike's visit. As a consequence, their time together was unusually quiet. The conversation didn't perk up until Fonnie mentioned that the president of Myerson Corporation was coming to lunch the next day.

"Old man Myerson himself? Coming here? How in the world did that come about?"

"He is not an old man. He's younger than I am. My brother and I went to school with him. And since he's in town, I thought it only hospitable to invite him over. Any objections?"

"No. Of course not. If you want to have an old—I mean, a former—boyfriend over, that's fine with me."

"Good. The only reason I'm telling you is so you won't barge in to grab a bite to eat while we're reminiscing."

"Gotcha. I'll plan on having lunch in town tomorrow."

THE NEXT MORNING Keisha arrived at five minutes before nine. Fonnie smiled in satisfaction; this girl knew the importance of punctuality.

The morning sped by quickly. While Fonnie soaked in the tub, Keisha ran the vacuum cleaner, and set the table for lunch. Fonnie picked out a soft pink blouse and dark ruby-colored pants to wear, and at the same time,

she framed questions in her mind she intended to ask
Dale Myerson. Lastly, Keisha curled, puffed, and teased
her client's red hair.

Just as Keisha was leaving for Barker's Buffet to pick
up the ordered lunch, the phone rang. She answered it.
It was Dale Myerson. Keisha handed the phone to Fonnie
and waited to see if the luncheon was still on or not.

Fonnie listened and responded intermittently, "Yes,
I understand." Pause. "Of course, no problem." Pause.
"Yes, that will be fine, Dale. I'll see you both soon then."

"Both?"

Fonnie nodded. "Dale is bringing his vice-president,
Ms. Franklin, with him. Seems that they're due for a
meeting with their lawyers at two and they'll have to
leave right from here."

"So much for your planned tete-a-tete. I'm sorry."

"Don't be. This may work out better than I thought."
Fonnie waved her cane at Keisha. "So get gone—and
double our order. That Franklin woman is pretty big,
probably a hefty eater."

To FONNIE, the introductions, the amenities, and the
chitchat took much too long. She had ordered cold cuts,
cheeses, various breads and spreads, so lunch could be a
"make your own sandwich" affair with a fruit plate for
dessert. Dale was munching on his Dagwood style con-
coction and between bites chattering on about the Myerson
Corporation, how he had landfill sites throughout a three-
state area, and the large number of jobs the sites generated.

Lanie Franklin nibbled away at her rye and Gouda,
interrupting now and again with precise figures such as,
"the Groverton landfill will have a solid waste disposal
capacity of nineteen million cubic yards."

That sounded like an awful lot of banana peels and shredded paper to Fonnie, but she had no idea what it actually meant. She did notice, however, that Lanie had omitted the word "proposed" when she described the Groverton site, as if there was no question about its fulfillment.

Fonnie saw that as her chance to jump in. "But what about the demonstrations against your proposed landfill? I understand there are some safety issues that need to be addressed."

"Nonsense," the vice-president answered before Dale could swallow his last mouthful. "Your so-called concerned citizens are nothing more than rabble rousers. There is absolutely no basis to their claims. Which is why we're meeting with our lawyers this afternoon to put a stop to it."

Fonnie studied the woman before her with grudging admiration. She's even more formidable in person than on TV, Fonnie thought. I can see how she's risen so high despite the odds of being black and a woman. But I'll be darned if she's going to intimidate me.

"If there's no basis for their safety-violation claims," Fonnie asked, "then why do you need a passel of lawyers?"

Dale choked, swallowed hard, took a long sip of iced tea, then managed a loud laugh. "I wouldn't say we have a *passel* of lawyers. Only what we need to get the job done. And the job right now is to allay the unfounded fears of the good citizens of Groverton."

"Unfounded?"

"Yes, completely unfounded. Fonnie, you've known me since we were kids. Can you actually believe I would run a company that purposely put people in danger?"

Fonnie shook her head. "No. Not purposely. But profit is a powerful motive—one that might tempt a businessman to cut corners, cover up, skew inspections."

Lanie shoved back from the table. "Are you suggesting that the Myerson Corporation would put profit over safety?"

Before Fonnie had a chance to answer, Dale spoke up, "Of course not, Lanie. She's not suggesting any such thing. Fonnie's always had a teasing sense of humor. In high school she liked to keep the student council members on their toes by asking such questions as, 'Why isn't *The Grapes of Wrath* in the school library?' or 'Were the football concession-stand receipts being accurately reported?'" He took a final swipe across his lips with his napkin and gave Fonnie his biggest smile. "I remember the time you hinted that some stolen band instruments were actually an insurance scam. You really had the principal on the hot seat for a while. Of course, nothing ever came of it."

"Nothing ever came of it because he threatened to put the label of 'agitator' on my record. And since I wanted to get into nursing school, I decided to keep my mouth shut from then on." Fonnie reached for a slice of apple, but kept her gaze straight on Dale's face. "I never tried to put anybody on the *hot seat.* I just asked legitimate questions to which I expected answers. I still do. The difference now is that I don't have to shut up in fear of getting a black mark on my record. So my question still stands. If your company has no history of safety violations, why do you need lawyers to put a stop to the demonstrations? All you need to do is open your records to the public. If there are no problems, the demonstrators will quietly fade into the woodwork and disappear."

"My dear Mrs. Beachum," Lanie Franklin reached over and patted Fonnie's hand as if correcting a recalcitrant child, "lay people, such as yourself, have a tendency to oversimplify business matters. Of course we have nothing to hide, but one doesn't open up records for public scrutiny. That would be naive." She dropped her napkin on the table and stood. "It's been a delightful lunch. Thank you so much for allowing me to join you. Can I help you clear the table before we go?"

Fonnie shook her head, "Thank you, but no. I can manage." She turned to Dale. "I know you're in a hurry, but with all our reminiscing, I haven't even told you my real reason for inviting you over."

Dale had half risen to his feet and now abruptly sat down. "Real reason?"

Lanie Franklin sat back down and gave Fonnie a wary look. "Real reason?"

"Yes. I thought you might be interested in the woman whose body was found at your landfill site. You see, she was a friend of mine." Fonnie had almost said *dear* friend, but was afraid that would be stretching the truth too much.

"I had no idea," Dale said. "All I heard was that she was one of the demonstrators. I don't even recall the name. Do you know anything about her, Lanie?"

"No. No, I don't. Wasn't her name Hanner, or something like that?"

"Hauner. Christine Hauner. I'm surprised that neither of you even seemed interested in the case. You didn't mention it, didn't ask how I, as a town resident, felt about it. Isn't solving a murder more important than silencing demonstrators?"

Dale spread his hands and shrugged his shoulders.

"Of course. But it's a police case. Nothing to do with us or our company."

"We hate that you've lost an old friend," Lanie said, "but then she had no business being there in the first place. People who join reckless demonstration groups should realize the danger they're putting themselves in."

"And why should a peaceful protest march be dangerous?" Fonnie was mad now, and she didn't try to hide it. "If I had two good legs, I might have been out there marching too. And Dale, if you had a shred of decency, you would put all your company's resources behind solving this case and catching the murderer before you did one more thing about that precious landfill."

"You can't talk to him like that!" Lanie jumped up so quickly her chair tipped over and crashed to the floor. She let it stay there. "Come on, Dale. We've got to go."

Dale stood up slowly. "I'm sorry about your friend. But there's nothing I can do to help. We have to leave it up to the police."

After she had escorted them to the door, Fonnie collapsed on the sofa. Tears slid down her cheeks, got caught in her wrinkles, slipped down inside the neck of her blouse. "They don't care. They don't care a bit." She recalled Dale's last words at the table. Well, I'm not going to leave it up to the police—not totally, anyway.

BEBE STUDIED HER MAIL as she unlocked her front door. The letter that interested her most was from the Environmental Defense League. She ripped open the top of the envelope, unable to hold her curiosity in check until she got to her desk and the letter opener. However, before she had a chance to read more than a few words, she heard a knock.

She held the letter behind her back as she answered the door. She was glad to see Neil, but at the same time she wished he had given her a few minutes to read the letter. Bebe wasn't sure she wanted to share its contents with him since he had suggested that CATWAG ought to back off from its demands.

Neil held high a bottle of Chardonnay and gave her a silly grin. "A jug of wine, a loaf of bread and thou." He laughed. "I don't remember the rest, but you get the point."

Bebe couldn't help but smile. "It's a good thing you teach art, not English Lit. Actually, I do remember the next lines. Suffice it to say, it has something to do with paradise. But since I'm serving crackers and not bread, I think we're safe. Come in. Make yourself comfortable while I get some glasses." She motioned to the recliner with her right hand, while her left hand fingered the thick envelope.

Her debate with herself about whether or not to show Neil the letter was short-lived. She soon realized she couldn't stand to wait much longer to know its contents. So after she loaded a tray with glasses and snacks, she placed the letter right on top.

"Would you like some news to go along with your jug of wine?"

"Good news?"

"I don't know yet. It's from the defense league. Maybe they've come up with a plan to stall Myerson."

"So I'll pour and you read."

Bebe started at the beginning. "To Citizens Against Toxic Waste At Groverton. From—"

"We know who it's from. What do they say?"

Bebe looked up from the letter, reached for her glass of wine and took a sip. "I'm not sure I should read it to you. After all, you're not an official member of CATWAG."

"I'm a member in spirit. That's what counts, isn't it?"

"I guess so." She picked up a Triscuit and a piece of cheddar, the letter momentarily forgotten as her mind took a U-turn to their earlier telephone conversation. "Do you really think we could be in danger—that Mrs. Hauner's death was a warning to us?"

Neil shrugged his shoulders. "It's possible. It might be a good idea for CATWAG to lie low for awhile. At least until the police make an arrest."

"But if we do that, we lose our momentum and possibly the entire battle." She took another sip of wine. "You know, I wish we were having this…" She hesitated and swept her hand over the tray, "this repast under more pleasant circumstances. I think I would really enjoy it."

"We will," Neil said. "When all this mess is over, I'll invite you to my place and we'll have a repast with wine and bread and repartee. In the meantime, I'll look up that paradise ending you mentioned and see what other ingredients I might need. Sound good?"

"Sounds fine to me. I only hope you like poetry." Bebe gave a long sigh. "But now to the matter at hand." She picked up the letter. "Dear so and so, blah, blah, blah. Here we go. 'We feel our best course of action would be to file a petition against the state's Division of Water Quality, for their issuance of a permit to Myerson Corporation. The petition will contend the proposed landfill would have a significant and adverse impact on the health and well-being of the members of CATWAG and of the residents of the city and county of Groverton, North Carolina. This will be based on the following concerns: 1) The proposed landfill will cause odors, noise, dust, increase in truck traffic, and other nuisance factors. 2) The proposed landfill will have a disproportionate impact on low income and minority families, since it is located in an area of the county where they live. 3) The proposed landfill is located in the flood plain adjacent to Tillent's Creek and this will directly affect the water quality in the Tillent Creek watershed.'"

Bebe paused, and Neil spoke up. "Now we're getting someplace. But I remember the company saying the landfill would have a waterproof lining so nothing could escape into the ground water."

"That's what they claim. But they've claimed that in other areas and investigations have proved that dangerous chemicals can leak out of their waterproof linings. In one county the ground water around the Myerson site was found to contain chemicals from pesticides, heavy metals, and solvents. The worst part is that the county health director suspects there could be birth defects and stillbirths if pregnant women drink the contaminated water."

"Really?"

"Really. This is serious business we're talking about." Bebe rattled the letter in her hand. "Let's see what else they say. '4) The proposed landfill will have a significant and adverse impact on fish, wildlife, and their habitat. 5) The Myerson Corporation has stated they plan to import garbage from other counties and even from out of state. The citizens of Groverton have no way of knowing what dangerous chemicals may be brought into their county and over their roads. It's true that Groverton County needs a new landfill, but its citizens object strongly to being a dumping ground for other areas. 6) The safety of Myerson Corporation has been called into question in several of their other landfills. Because of the above facts, we will petition that the permit issued to Myerson Corporation be rescinded.'"

Bebe stopped reading to go back over the six points in her mind. "I don't think points one, two, or four will create much of a stir, but the other three certainly ought to raise enough red flags to get an injunction."

"Seems like. Is that all they had to say?"

"They close with this advice. 'We suggest you solicit other organizations to stand with you in the fight, such as The League of Women Voters, the Sierra Club, and if possible, the newspapers.'" Bebe carefully put the letter back in its envelope. "Well, what do you think?"

"I think you're going to be bullheaded enough to charge ahead—no matter what I say about possible danger."

EIGHT

AFTER HER GUESTS had gone, Fonnie slipped on an old-fashion bib apron. It was one of several she had bought at the nursing-home craft fair. It had big pockets in front and the tie in back had been replaced with velcro, so she could easily fasten it with one hand. She then busied herself clearing the table and putting the leftover food in the refrigerator. It was a slow process since she had to load everything on her tea cart, push it slowly across the room, and then unload it. She was surprised that more of the offering hadn't been eaten. So I was wrong about Ms. Franklin's appetite, she thought. Since she's as big as an Amazon, I expected her to eat like one. No problem. I'm sure Brian will finish everything off as his bedtime snack.

Fonnie tried to put the Myerson executives and their uncaring attitude out of her mind as she concentrated on her next step. She had wanted to ask Lanie some questions about the scene at the landfill site before the body was discovered, but that chance vanished when their party came to an abrupt end. Surely Brian knows more than he's telling me, she thought. I'll have another go at him when he comes in.

A firm knock on the front door ended her musings. She took her time going across the kitchen, through the den, and down the hall. She figured if it was a salesman, he'd give up and leave before she got there. Before she opened the door, she dug in her apron pocket and was relieved to find her phone nestled there under a wad of tissues. She was trying to do better about keeping her phone handy as Brian had insisted, but that wasn't always easy.

Fonnie started to open the door when she remembered another of Brian's admonitions of keeping the chain in place. She hadn't replaced it after her guests left so she did it now.

There had been no further knocks after the first one, and since she had taken so long to get to the door, Fonnie expected to look out onto an empty porch. To her surprise, when she peered out under the chain, she looked into the face of a playful bear surrounded by crimson letters that read *Groverton Cubs*. She raised her eyes enough to see who was wearing the high school sweatshirt, and another playful face smiled at her.

"Mrs. Beachum?"

"Yes."

"I'm Tyrone Riggs. Keisha's brother. She said you needed someone to do yard work. I'd be glad to help if you want me to."

"Of course. I should have been expecting you. Keisha said she would ask you to come by. Let me shut the door a moment while I unhook this silly chain." Fonnie then opened the door and swung it wide. "Come on in."

"No Ma'am. I'd just as soon get to work. The days are getting shorter and I'll only have a couple of hours before dark. I brought my own rake and stuff. Any particular place you want me to start?"

"Better do the front first so the neighbors won't be

getting up a petition against me. I guess Keisha told you the yard was in bad shape."

"Yes ma'am," Tyrone said. His grin showed perfect white teeth against a bronze background. "Actually she said it was a huge mess. But then, Keisha always does tend to exaggerate."

Fonnie laughed. "In this case, I think she was right. Just do what you can today. The broken limbs can be stacked by the driveway and the leaves raked to the curb. The city crews will come by and pick them up."

"Will do." Tyrone took the two porch steps in one long stride, then turned back. "It's mighty pretty out today. Why don't you come sit in your porch swing?"

Until that moment, Fonnie had taken no notice of the day's weather. It had been a cold fall. She'd gotten accustomed to the chilly winds, the nasty rains. But today the sun was bright, the sky clear, and a soft warm breeze gently rocked her swing. "What a marvelous idea. I'll just get my sweater. Are you sure you won't mind if I watch you work?"

"Not at all. But don't expect me to keep up a scintillating conversation."

"Young man, I doubt if you even know what a scintillating conversation is." Fonnie paused as she opened the door and said, more to herself than to the boy in her yard, "And it's been so long since I've had one, I doubt I could remember the technique."

Fonnie used her cane to propel the swing, laid her head back, and reveled in the warm air, the sound of swishing leaves, the occasional whiff of pine sap where a branch had broken off the evergreen. Calmness settled over her like a down comforter. In spite of everything, life was good. Her eyes closed, her head lolled, her breathing turned into a gentle snore.

Several minutes later, her apron pocket began to twitch and wail. Fonnie woke up immediately, but it took her quite a while to orient herself to where she was and that the racket was coming from her person. When she finally answered the phone, it was with a gruff 'Hello,' as if she wanted to kill the messenger for interrupting a beautiful nap.

"Gram, what in the world took you so long to answer the phone?"

Fonnie was wide awake now, and wasn't about to take any crap from Brian. "Now don't you accuse me of not having my phone nearby. It was right here in my pocket, but you woke me from a nap. I was having a scintillating conversation with someone in my dream and I didn't want to leave."

"A what kind of conversation?"

"Never mind. I'm back to my normal dull, but cheery self. So what is it you want?"

"Two things. First, I wondered how your date went this afternoon."

"Terrible. But I don't want to talk about it now. What else?"

"All right. Secondly, I have a date tonight myself, and I certainly hope it goes better than yours did."

Fonnie sat up straighter and smiled into the phone. "A date? That's nice. Anybody I know?"

"Nope. She's another police rookie."

"Does she have a name?" Fonnie imagined she heard Brian give a small groan.

"Hazel Parker. She's tall, pretty, and does better at the shooting range than I do."

"Sounds like someone I could like. What are your plans?"

"Nothing special. Just dinner and a movie. But I may be in late. That okay?"

"Sure. Don't worry about me. But aren't you coming home to change out of your uniform?"

"Don't have to. I have extra clothes in my locker here. And, Gram, leave the chain off the kitchen door when you go to bed. I'll be coming in there."

"Sure. Have a good time. Bye." Fonnie patted the phone as she replaced it in her apron pocket. Now that's nice. Brian has a girlfriend.

She shivered slightly and realized the sun had lost some of its warmth. She pushed herself up and looked around for Tyrone. He was raking the last of the leaves from under the maple tree. The ground was bare and brown. The boy was sweating. She called out to him. "How about taking a break? I've got some iced tea in the fridge."

He swiveled around, grinned. "Sounds good. This is about all I can do today, anyway. Maybe I can finish Saturday. I have ball practice tomorrow, and a game Friday night."

"That'll be fine. At least the front yard is presentable again. Come on in."

This time Tyrone accepted the invitation. He stomped and wiped his feet on the mat, then waited for her to precede him.

"There's a bathroom down the hall on the right. You can wash up there. Then come out to the kitchen."

Fonnie slid the tea cart to the refrigerator, reached for the tea, then decided to bring out the left-over sandwich plate as well. She had the table set with glasses, utensils, paper plates, and napkins by the time Tyrone found his way to the kitchen. "I took a wrong turn," he explained. "I ended up in your library and started looking at some of the books. Sorry about that."

Actually, Fonnie was delighted to find out that Tyrone was a reader, as well as a football player, an artist, and a great yard man. "Don't be sorry. If you see any you want to take home, feel free to do so."

"Thanks. But I don't have much time to read right now. Maybe later."

Fonnie motioned to him to sit down. The chair that Lanie Franklin had knocked over still lay on its side, but Fonnie had chosen to ignore it since she didn't feel safe in stooping down to pick it up. Tyrone, however, stepped around the table and righted the chair, then plopped himself down in it. "What did you do— have a barroom brawl in here?"

"Something like that." She gestured toward the plate of bread and cold cuts. "And this is what's left of the party menu before the brawl broke out. Help yourself. My grandson just called and said he was going out to dinner and wouldn't be home until late. I certainly can't eat all this."

Tyrone didn't bother to demur. "Raking leaves can certainly instigate an appetite," he said, and proceeded to slather a piece of crusty bread with mayo and mustard, and to pile on sliced beef, turkey and salami.

"Yes, it certainly seems to have instigated your appetite. But what has me curious is—what has instigated your propensity to utilize such lofty terminology in your scintillating conversations?"

Tyrone barely managed to swallow without choking on his laughter. "So you've noticed? Good. That means my studying the thesaurus has paid off. Keisha said I had to increase my vocabulary for my SAT. So you be sure and tell her I've been working on it."

"I'll do that, if you promise not to inundate me with superfluous syllables."

Since Tyrone again had a full mouth, he simply nodded in agreement. After his second sandwich, he wiped his mouth and slid his chair back. "Better save some room for dinner tonight."

Fonnie walked with him to the door. "See you Saturday, then?"

"Sure thing. Now be sure and fasten the chain when I'm gone. You're not afraid to stay here all alone at night?"

"Don't be silly. Why should I be afraid?"

The wind rasped against the windows, clawing its way through cracks where putty had been chiseled away by passing years. The beautiful fall day had turned into a cold, wintry, eerie night. The window panes didn't actually rattle; it was more of a tinkle, a warning bell that the house had been neglected too long. Fonnie wondered if Tyrone might be a handy man as well as a yard man. Maybe she could get him to caulk the windows for her.

She pushed herself up from the recliner, grasped her four-pronged friend, and said, "Come on, Amigo, let's close the drapes and keep out the bogeyman." Fonnie couldn't remember when she'd started talking to her quad cane, but she was no longer embarrassed to do it. Brian had teased her about it, but she explained that the cane was her companion and she would talk to it if she wanted to.

She was working her way around the den when another noise intruded into her space. It seemed to come from upstairs. Brian's room? Amy's old room?

Fonnie stood still, listened. There it was again. A step? Impossible. It had to be the wind. Maybe a draft was flopping around some of Brian's study notes. He might even have left his window open. Brian was a fresh-air fiend. Well, that was fine during the summer, but not when the temperature at night was dipping into the thirties and forties. She would have to speak to him about it. He'd be home in a few hours and until then she'd just ignore it. There was no way she was going to attempt going up the stairs to investigate.

Tyrone's last question leapt into her mind again. *You're not afraid to stay here all alone at night?* Of course she was afraid—but she wasn't going to admit it to anybody. She just hoped Brian's date wouldn't keep him out too late.

NINE

FONNIE AWOKE IN A SNIT. She was mad at herself because she had allowed the noises of a creaky old house to frighten her. She was mad at the wind because it had scattered Tyrone's carefully raked leaves back over the front yard. She was mad at Brian because he had gotten in late and left early. She had heard him in the kitchen humming a tune that sounded suspiciously happy, then she heard him slam out the door without even poking his head into her bedroom to see if she was awake or even to check if she was alive. I could have had another stroke during the night, she thought, and he wouldn't know—or care.

Immediately she realized her wretched mood had gone too far. Brian often had to leave early, depending on his shift, or his assignment for the day. It had nothing to do with her. And he knew Keisha would be coming in soon, so there was nothing to worry about.

But Fonnie was still irritated. She'd wanted to quiz him about his date, and she had thought of more questions about the demonstration. Both would have to wait until he got in tonight—if he came in tonight.

She was huddled on the den sofa with her third cup of coffee, still in her nightgown and housecoat, when Keisha knocked on the front door. Fonnie struggled to her feet and headed for the door. Maybe I ought to give

Keisha a key to the back door, she thought, and leave it unchained so she can get in without me getting up. I didn't give Christine a key, but I did get up and make sure the door was unlocked so she could come on in. But what if there came a morning when she couldn't get up? Fonnie felt despondency dropping over her again like a black cloud. Even the morning's bright sunshine and Keisha's beaming face couldn't dispel Fonnie's gloom. It further irritated her that Keisha seemed to take no notice that her client wasn't happy.

The girl slipped off her jacket, flung it over the coat rack, and headed for the broom closet. After a few moments burrowing around in its contents she came out with the dust mop, some rags torn from old sheets, a bright yellow can of lemon-scented furniture polish, and the hand-held Dirt Devil. "Now for some serious cleaning." She turned to Fonnie. "While you're getting dressed, I'll start in the living room. I know you don't use it much, but there's no use letting the dust take up permanent residence."

Fonnie stared at her aide. "Aren't you going to help me?"

"Help you what?"

"Get dressed."

Keisha looked puzzled. "You've been dressing yourself for weeks. And you had a bath yesterday. Can't dry out your skin with a bath every day. Of course, I'll help you pick out something to wear if that's what you mean."

"Never mind." Fonnie turned abruptly and headed for her bedroom. "I can manage quite well, thank you."

Keisha shrugged and aimed her arsenal toward the living room. Thirty minutes later the room sparkled and glittered and smelled like a Florida orchard. Fonnie came out of her room without the least bit of sparkle or glitter and smelled like Ben-Gay.

Keisha took a deep sniff. "That stuff may not do much for your arthritis, but it certainly will keep the mosquitoes at a distance."

Fonnie tried to think of a smart comeback and failed.

Fonnie's lack of retort finally got Keisha's attention. "What's the matter? Didn't you and Tyrone get along yesterday? You don't have to pay him if his work isn't satisfactory. I know the wind played havoc last night but he'll take care of everything the next time he comes."

"It isn't Tyrone. In fact, I liked him a great deal. He's a hard worker and good company and," Fonnie allowed herself a slight smile as she added, "he has an excellent vocabulary."

Keisha sighed in relief. "Good. But something's bothering you. What is it?"

Fonnie honestly didn't know how to answer. What was bothering her? It was all so vague, so shadowy— nothing she could put into words. If she wasn't such a sensible person, she might have admitted to a foreboding, an augur pointing to some danger, either to herself or to a loved one. So instead of answering the question, she ignored it. "Nothing that another cup of coffee won't help. Could you get my cup from the den?"

While Fonnie made her way to the kitchen, Keisha retrieved the coffee mug and poured the last of the coffee from the pot. "There you are," she said. "Now when you finish your coffee you can load the washing machine while I clean the bathrooms."

Fonnie glared at Keisha. "What do you mean—I can load the washing machine? What do you think I'm paying you to do?" Fonnie's foul mood had now turned downright ugly, but if Keisha noticed, she didn't let on.

The aide smiled, pulled out a chair, sat down opposite her old friend, and said sweetly, "You're not paying me. Amy is. And her instructions to me were to try to make you more independent. And so a good start in that direction is for you to load the washer, pour in the detergent, and twirl the dial. We'll work on moving the clothes from the washer to the dryer another day."

But Fonnie wasn't about to let it end there. "And what, pray tell, are you going to be doing while I'm standing on my head lifting clothes from the basket and probably falling on my ass?"

"As I said, I'm going to be cleaning the bathrooms. But I'll hear you if you fall and will be right there to pick you up."

Fonnie searched for a telltale smirk or a hint of a smile on Keisha's face. There was none. "You're serious." Fonnie could hardly believe it. Keisha—sweet, funny, lovable Keisha— had turned on her. "I didn't have to do my own laundry at Springwillow. I don't see why I should do it now." Fonnie saw a flicker of hurt in Keisha's eyes, a flicker that was quickly replaced with determination.

"You know what's wrong with you, Fonnie?" Keisha's voice was soft, but the words stabbed Fonnie deep in her soul.

"There's not a thing wrong with me that a new body wouldn't cure."

Keisha went on as if Fonnie had not said a thing. "You're suffering from slave mentality. My daddy used to preach on that."

In spite of her anger, Fonnie jerked to attention. Her

grip tightened on her cane so much her knuckles showed white. But Keisha's sincerity made her sit up and listen.

"After Abraham Lincoln freed our ancestors, some of them longed for the safety of their masters' plantations, for their little cabins, for the handouts from the big house. That was slave mentality. The thought of making their own way in the world was too much to handle.

"You're a Bible scholar," Keisha went on. "I'm sure you remember how the Israelites reacted in the Sinai after they left their bondage in Egypt. They actually complained about the manna God sent them, and recalled what good things they had to eat while they were slaves in Egypt. They were willing to give up freedom for leeks and onions and garlic. That was slave mentality. That's what I mean about you. You have your freedom here, Fonnie, but freedom means doing your own laundry.

"True, you didn't have to wash your own clothes in the nursing home. You didn't have to cook. You didn't have to remember to take your meds." Keisha was on a roll now. "You also had to get up when you were told to, go to meals when they were served, turn lights out at a specified time, share a room with another person. Now are you really willing to trade your freedom here just so you won't have to load a washing machine?"

Keisha's laugh finally broke out. "I'd better be careful. Next thing you know I'll be pounding on the pulpit."

"Okay, okay. I get the picture. I'll do the wash, I'll wash the dishes, I'll even wash my own backside, if only you'll shut up."

Keisha pulled an imaginary zipper across her lips, and Fonnie lifted a dirty sheet from the laundry hamper.

As the morning wore on, Fonnie's mood improved.

Keisha had moved from the first floor bathrooms to the one upstairs. Fonnie decided that maybe she really could wash the few dishes that had accumulated since yesterday. She scooted a high stool from the bar to the front of the sink, carefully climbed aboard, and filled the sink with suds. She found she could hold a dish or a cup with her weak left hand while scrubbing furiously with her right hand. She was feeling good about the whole thing when she heard Keisha come into the room, pause, and then come up behind her. Fonnie turned her head and caught the aide's wide grin. "Feeling pretty smart, aren't you?" Fonnie asked.

"Not half as smart as you're feeling, I bet. But don't overdo it. There's another day coming." Keisha silently rinsed the dishes as Fonnie continued to wash them. When they finished, Keisha helped Fonnie down from her stool and motioned to the table. "Want to talk about what's troubling you now? I'll pour us some iced tea."

"I guess it's frustration. I'm trying to learn more about the landfill controversy, which in turn might help me understand what happened to poor Christine. My meeting with Myerson and his lackey was totally unproductive. I would love to talk to someone from CATWAG, but I don't know who to contact."

"Bebe Englehook. She's the backbone of the organization."

"You know her?"

"No, but Tyrone does. I only learned that Tuesday afternoon when I was talking to his counselor. She made the remark he ought to work toward getting a college art scholarship, instead of painting protest signs. When I asked Tyrone about it, he admitted to making the signs for Bebe and her cohorts to carry at the demonstration.

He was very impressed with her and her zeal. I'm sure she'd be glad to talk to you. From what I've seen of her on the news, she's not shy about sharing her views."

Fonnie nodded her head. "Excellent idea. I'll call her this afternoon."

"She runs Second Chance Book Store. You can find the number in the phone book."

TEN

THINGS WERE QUIET at the bookstore, so Bebe took some time to respond to the letter from the Defense League. She agreed with their suggested strategy, then added information about the body found at the landfill and the investigation. *"Unfortunate as it is, this incident will buy us some time to deal with Myerson."* As she reread that last sentence on the computer screen, she realized how unfeeling it sounded. She backspaced and tried again. *"This tragic event will, no doubt, delay Myerson's plans. But it may work to our advantage."* She still wasn't satisfied, but didn't want to spend more time on the letter. She hurriedly finished it and started the printer. Her mind left the Defense League behind, and moved on to the tragic event.

Bebe wished she knew more about Christine Hauner: why had she attended CATWAG meetings if she didn't intend to join? What, if any, incriminating knowledge did she have about the Myerson Corporation? And was her death really meant as a warning? But how can I find out anything further? The TV and newspapers keep repeating the same information: her age, her employer, that she moved here from southern Virginia.

She ran the few facts around in her head. They were of no help. She had to learn more. The ringing of the phone brought her mind back to the bookstore and back to her life before Myerson, before protests, before a found body. She hoped it was either a customer or Neil. She didn't feel up to anybody else.

"Second Chance Book Store. Bebe here. How may I help you?" She listened carefully to the caller's request. "Of course, I'd be glad to talk to you about our organization. What did you say your name was?" She reached for the notebook she kept by the phone. "Mrs. Fonnie Beachum. Well, Mrs. Beachum, I'll be at the store until about four. Could you come by here?" Bebe nodded from time to time while Mrs. Beachum explained her physical condition and that she was unable to visit the bookstore. But when the woman asked Bebe to come to her house, she tried to think of a nice way to refuse. She was always glad to talk about CATWAG, but she couldn't be running all over town doing private interviews.

It wasn't until Mrs. Beachum mentioned that they had a mutual friend in Tyrone Riggs, that she reconsidered. "You know Tyrone? Isn't he just the nicest boy?" They chatted a few minutes about Tyrone, but that wasn't enough to convince Bebe to make the trip across town. After all, she asked herself, what good could a crippled old woman do our organization? She certainly couldn't march if we staged another protest.

But when her caller mentioned another name, Bebe became really interested. "You knew Christine Hauner?" Bebe listened carefully as Mrs. Beachum explained that Christine worked for her.

"I was just thinking about poor Christine," Bebe said. "In fact, I was thinking I would like CATWAG to have some kind of memorial service for her." Bebe took a deep breath and wondered where in the world that crazy idea had come from. But maybe it wasn't so crazy after all. She decided to go for it. "Perhaps you would like to help with the service." Mrs. Beachum declared that, indeed, she would like to participate. "Good, then I'll come to your house after I close the store and we can discuss it."

Bebe nodded in satisfaction. So Christine, I'm finally going to learn more about you.

FONNIE IMMEDIATELY LIKED Bebe. It took courage, Fonnie thought, for a short woman to wear a dirndl midi-skirt and an Eton jacket. And her heavy brown brogans completed an outfit that spoke of a comfortable and confident woman. Fonnie was glad she had heated water for tea rather than making coffee. Bebe was definitely a tea drinker.

Over green tea and gingersnaps, Bebe answered Fonnie's many questions about CATWAG's objections to Myerson. Fonnie shook her head in bewilderment. "It's hard to believe Dale Myerson would run such a company."

"I know. He actually seems like a nice man. But nice men have been known to be greedy. And I'm afraid that's what happened to him." Bebe sipped her tea. "Now let's change the subject and talk about Christine."

The two women shared all they knew about the murdered woman. They soon realized it was precious little.

"I guess Christine is going to remain an enigma," Bebe said. "Not that it really matters. I was just so curious about her connection to Myerson. But I guess we've hit a dead end, and I might as well be going."

Fonnie shook her head. "We're not at a dead end, and you're not going anywhere. We still have the memorial service to plan."

"Oh, that. It was a crazy thought. I don't know why I even mentioned it."

"Not crazy at all. In fact, it was downright inspired. That's how we're going to get answers to our questions." Bebe raised her eyebrows, but before she could say anything, Fonnie went on. "Let's schedule the memorial for Sunday afternoon. I'll leave the place and details up to you. My part will be to plan the interview questions."

"Interview questions? What interview?"

"The interviews that we—that is, you and your colleagues, are going to have with everybody we invite to the service. That will include people at the Home Health Agency, the Whitehall house, her neighbors, the people where she went to church—if she did, where she shopped, where she got her hair done." Fonnie paused. "No. Scratch that. She hadn't been inside a hair salon for years. But she had to buy gas, uniforms, whatever."

Bebe started nodding her head as Fonnie warmed up to her subject. "We'll have flyers made—tasteful flyers, announcing the memorial service. Tyrone could design them since he's an artist. We'll hand-distribute them, and when we do, we'll ask discreet questions about Christine: her habits, her friends, and whatever else I can come up with."

"I get it," Bebe said, "and we'll ask if any of them would care to say a few words at the service. And since CATWAG is sponsoring the service, we can ask if she ever mentioned us or ever made any comments about the landfill."

"Yes. But, like I said, we'll have to be discreet. We don't want to appear to be prying."

"Despite the fact that's exactly what we'll be doing."

Bebe munched thoughtfully on a cookie while Fonnie started scratching down notes. "We don't have much time," Bebe said. "Only two days."

"It can be done. I have full confidence in you."

Bebe laughed. "That's easy for you to say. You're going to be sitting here in your recliner while I'm out there in the trenches."

Fonnie's face darkened. "Yes, but, believe me, I'd rather be out there in the trenches with you."

"I'm sorry. I didn't mean—" Bebe stumbled over her words. "I didn't think how that sounded."

"That's all right. Someday, I'll regale you with all my adventures when I was able to fight in the trenches, to battle for the underdog, to right society's wrongs."

Bebe held up a hand. "Fine. Fine. But now back to the plan at hand. I can get Ginny, a friend of mine, to keep the bookstore open tomorrow and Saturday. I'll call a meeting tonight in my home for some of the most dedicated CATWAG members, the ones I know I can trust, who can handle the assignment. We'll plan where to go, and what to ask. That's where you come in by supplying us with some good discreet questions. We'll leave the neighbors for Saturday, since they'll more likely be home then. Then we'll meet here Saturday night and put all our information together. How does that sound?"

"Fantastic." Fonnie did some quick thinking about how she could get Brian out of the house Saturday evening. She knew he wouldn't approve of their plan at all. Maybe he'll have another date with Hazel, she thought. At least, I could suggest it.

Bebe jerked Fonnie's mind back to the task at hand. "I'll arrange to use the auditorium at the West End Re-

creation Facility for the service. It should be available—
not much going on this time of year." She looked across
at Fonnie. "Do we serve refreshments? I've never done
a memorial before."

"It's a good way to keep people hanging around. And
when they hang around, they talk. So I say yes, we serve
refreshments, tastefully done, of course."

Fonnie glanced at the clock. It was nearly time for
Brian to come in, and she didn't relish the thought of
introducing Bebe to her cop grandson. "So, I guess
we've done all we can for now. Call me in the morning
and we'll go from there."

Bebe stood up, straightened her skirt, gave Fonnie a
firm handshake. "It's going to be a pleasure working
with you."

After Bebe left, Fonnie hurried to the computer to get
her jumbled thoughts in some kind of order. So much
was happening so fast.

October 18

    Bebe is a delightful person, but is she right
about Myerson? Or is she exaggerating the
possible dangers of the landfill? Could I be wrong
about an old school chum? Of course, Dale wasn't
a chum and I know nothing about him between
then and now. But the important thing now is
whether Myerson is right or wrong. What I want
to know is what Christine knew or thought she
knew about the company. What triggered her ani-
mosity? Why did she question the purity of my
water? Did any of this result in her death?
    Maybe the Memorial Service is a crazy idea.

Can we hope to uncover any really pertinent information simply by talking to Christine's associates? And surely, the police have already done this. But sometimes people are more talkative with ordinary folks than with police. It's worth a try. What possible harm could come of it?

Fonnie heard Brian come in the kitchen door and almost immediately heard the refrigerator door open. She smiled as she clicked the print button. Her journal would have to wait. Now was her chance to act the inquisitor to Brian.

"Sorry, Gram. I don't know nothin'. Ain't saying nothin'."

"Fine. Then I ain't telling you nothin'."

Brain laughed as he crammed a piece of salami in his mouth. "You keep hanging around with me and you'll be able to talk to the best of the street gangs."

Fonnie smiled in spite of her irritation, then his words spun around in her head. "Street gangs? We have street gangs in Groverton?"

"Well, there's some kind of gang. Two more B & Es this week while the owners were gone. Took jewelry, electronics, silver—anything that's easy to hock."

"Same MO as my break-in?"

Brian laughed again. "You're getting pretty good at police talk too." He dunked a piece of whole wheat in the toaster and poured a glass of milk. "Yep. Same modus operandi. They're quick and slick."

"And the loot disappears to never-never land."

Brian nodded. "But they'll slip up one of these days. We'll get them and probably recover some of the goods. So don't give up on your silver yet."

"So you think I might see Leopold again?"

"It's possible. We've got lists out to all the pawn shops in the area. After all, a silver unicorn isn't something one sees every day. If he shows up, we'll be notified."

Fonnie hugged the thought that one day Leopold might again stand guard over her house. It made her feel just a little safer.

ELEVEN

IT WASN'T OFTEN in Fonnie's life that everything went according to plan. The next two days were exceptions. Bebe confirmed the site and time of the service; Tyrone designed the announcements and made a hundred copies; Fonnie wrote out a list of questions that each interviewer could modify according to the situation or the person responding. Bebe conscripted four intelligent, personable canvassers, besides herself, to visit people whom Christine had known, to invite them to the memorial service, and in the process, to suck up every bit of information about the dead woman they could. On Saturday, when Tyrone expressed a desire to join the ranks, Fonnie decided her yard maintenance could wait a few days.

It was now close to five-thirty. Brian had left for a dinner date, and Fonnie anxiously awaited the gathering of her coconspirators. When she saw the cars drive up, she swung the door wide and ushered everyone into the living room. Her living room had always been reserved for special occasions, and this was certainly one of them. It might almost be called the inaugural night of the Fonnie Beachum Detective Agency.

Bebe led the parade, followed by Patty, Doug, Isaac, Jennifer and Tyrone. Fonnie had only met the four middle ones that morning, but already they felt like close friends. They scattered around the spacious living room, plopping on the leather sofa, reclining in the wingback chairs, or making themselves comfortable on the floor while leaning against the fireplace.

Fonnie smiled at each one as they took their seats. She cleared her throat loudly to still the whispers and buzzing around the room. Having little success, she clapped her hands. That did the trick. "Now that I have your attention," she said, "I want to thank each of you for your help in our effort."

"You're welcome," Isaac answered, "But I'm still a little hazy about why we did what we did. Was all this necessary just to stage a little memorial service?"

"For someone we didn't even know?" Patty spoke from the far corner of the sofa. She'd slipped off her shoes, and was now hugging her knees. "What does this have to do with CATWAG and the landfill?"

"I guess I do owe you a more thorough explanation," Fonnie said. "Actually, you have been assisting in the Christine Hauner murder investigation. I assured the detective in charge that I would be willing to assist in anyway I could. After all, I did solve three murders that occurred at the Springwillow Nursing Home."

Eyebrows shot up, slumped bodies came to attention, a chorus of "O-oh" sounded throughout the room.

"That's right," Tyrone said. "My sister, Keisha, was working there at the time and she said Fonnie was a real hero."

Fonnie beamed at the attention, then waved her hand. "But enough of that. Let's get started on this case. As in any investigation, the first thing is to get the facts. And that's what you've been doing. So we'll go around the room and you'll tell what you've learned about Christine Hauner. Don't leave anything out. The simplest detail may be very important. I hope you took notes as you were instructed." Heads nodded, notebooks came out, eyes focused on their leader. "If no one has any objection, I'm going to record your remarks, so I can go over them again later." Fonnie held up a small tape recorder, placed it on the end table by her side, and pushed the start button.

While she was doing that, Tyrone leaned over and whispered something to Bebe. Bebe whispered something back. Fonnie tapped on the table with her knuckles, and stared at the two of them. "Can we get started now?"

"I'm sorry," Tyrone said. "I was just asking why Neil Vincent wasn't here. I assumed he'd be helping us."

Fonnie hadn't met Neil, but Bebe had told her about him identifying the body. "Yes, his input would have been valuable. Didn't you ask him to come, Bebe?"

"I asked him. He declined." Bebe paused as if debating whether to say anything else, then apparently decided to do so. "He said we were treading on dangerous ground—that Christine was probably killed because she knew too much and that the less we knew, the better."

Murmurs started around the room, which Fonnie stopped with a sharp, "Nonsense. The gentleman seems to have the backbone of a pollywog. So let's forget about him and get on with our business. Bebe, would you please begin?"

"All right." Bebe adjusted her reading glasses and consulted her notes. "I visited Mrs. Scoggins at the home health agency. Christine worked there for just over three years. She was considered a satisfactory employee. The client she had in the mornings prior to coming to Fonnie's had died from natural causes two weeks earlier. She had been doing afternoon duty with Mrs. Whitehall for about five months and the agency had heard no complaints about her work. Mrs. Scoggins visits in each client's home once a month and writes a report. During those visits she specifically asks the client and/or the family if they have any complaints about their aide. Since Mrs. Whitehall is mainly nonresponsive and since her son is seldom home, she spoke to the housekeeper and was told that Christine's work was fine." Bebe shifted her feet and went on. "There was no one else in the office except the secretary. All the aides and nurses work independently. So they don't really get to know each other. Mrs. Scoggins said that, as far as she knew, Christine was not friends with any of the other staff. Mrs. Scoggins said she would try to come to the memorial service and would post a notice, but she doubted if anyone else would come."

Bebe turned a page in her notebook. "I then went to the Whitehall home. The housekeeper, Mrs. Pruitt, was rather vague. She said that she usually used the time when Christine was there to shop, do errands, or just to rest. She said when Christine first started working there, she was fairly friendly, and sometimes after she finished with Mrs. Whitehall's bath, they would sit down together and have a cup of coffee. But in the past couple of months Christine had become more withdrawn, and seemed to be rather nervous." Bebe skimmed over her notes. "Oh yes, I thought this was interesting. Mrs. Pruitt said that one day, Mr. Whitehall came home unexpectedly in the middle of the afternoon and went in to see his mother. He apparently asked the aide to leave the room and Mrs. Pruitt said that Christine appeared very upset."

Fonnie interrupted with a question. "Did Mrs. Pruitt have any explanation, or did Christine explain why she was upset?"

"No. But when Mr. Whitehall left, Christine went back into the room and kept the door shut the rest of the afternoon."

"Was that unusual?" This time the question came from Patty. Fonnie was glad to see that her allies were really getting interested now.

"Yes," Bebe said. "According to Mrs. Pruitt, Christine usually left the bedroom door open after she finished the bath routine. Well, anyway, that's about it. I did go in the bedroom, and I spoke to Mrs. Whitehall. She must be in her nineties. She just kind of lies there. I think she can hear, but she doesn't respond to questions, and I don't know how much she's in touch with her surroundings or with reality." Bebe closed her notebook. "This was on Friday. I wanted to see Mr. Whitehall, so I went by his office, but I was told he was out of town on business. I went back to the house this morning, hoping to catch him, but Mrs. Pruitt said he was playing golf. She was baking cookies so she invited me into the kitchen while she worked. Such a lovely old house. They don't make big kitchens like that anymore."

Fonnie wasn't interested in architecture and interrupted with, "But did she say anything else about Christine?"

"Not really. But while I was there, a scruffy teenage boy came in and wanted to know where his grandpa was. He was really mad when Mrs. Pruitt told him about the golf game. The housekeeper tried to introduce us, said his name was Jerry, but the boy had the manners of a turnip. He ignored me and stalked out. Then she made the remark that Christine had taken a liking to Jerry, that he reminded her of her own boys. I left, but asked her to be sure and give Mr. Whitehall the flyer about the service. She said she would. That's it for me."

Fonnie nodded. "Good. Who wants to be next?" She looked over at the sofa.

Patty jerked up. "I will. Not much to report though."

"Let me be the judge of that. You just tell us the facts."

"Okay, sure. I called on two of her neighbors this morning. But you can hardly call them neighbors. It's a rural area, the houses are far apart. The first one was on the same side of the road, within sight of Christine's house, but not close enough to see much. Incidentally, we could tell for sure which one was Christine's house because the crime tape was still up. Anyway, the first house was a Latino couple, very nice, with a toddler. Their English wasn't perfect, but it was a whole lot better than my Spanish. The husband did most of the talking, said he had already spoken to the police. He said he and his wife didn't know Christine, just saw her coming and going. Said she seldom had visitors. He seemed confused about what a memorial service was. I'm not sure I explained it very well."

"Let me get this straight. He reported she seldom had visitors," Fonnie said. "Is that right?"

"Yeah. Well, he didn't say 'seldom' but that's what he meant."

"But doesn't that imply she *did* have some visitors—perhaps, rarely, but somebody did come to see her at times?"

Patty slid back into the sofa corner. "I guess so. Should I have quizzed him about it further? Asked the type of car and so on?"

"Don't worry about it. You did okay. I'll check later

with the police. They may already have that information. Now, what about the other neighbor?"

"Even less there. An old couple. They didn't know her or anything about her. You can't see her house from theirs. They'd heard she'd been killed, but they didn't seem too interested."

"That's odd," Bebe said.

Patty looked up in surprise. "What's odd?"

"Not being interested in a murder in your own neighborhood—even if they didn't know her. It's just human nature to be curious about murder and mayhem." Bebe turned to Fonnie. "Could it be they were afraid to say anything?"

"That's possible. We can check it out later." Fonnie's eyes went to the next person on the sofa. "Got anything for us, Doug?"

Doug sat up straight, ran a hand over his thinning hair, pushed his glasses back a fraction of an inch. He looked to be in his mid-forties, his body lean, his face vacuous. Fonnie imagined that joining CATWAG was probably the most exciting thing he'd ever done. He pulled a ballpoint pen from his jacket pocket and a legal-size yellow pad from the briefcase at his feet. "My assignment was to cover the places where Mrs. Hauner may have shopped. And I had exceptional luck. There's a Winn-Dixie near the road leading to her house. I actually had little hope of anybody knowing her even if she did shop there, but I was pleasantly surprised. I talked to the manager first and asked if I could post the notice about the memorial service. He agreed, and he told me Christine shopped there all the time, always cashed her paycheck there. According to him, she was quiet but friendly. He directed me to one of the cashiers who remembered waiting on her Friday evening. She said that Christine usually bought the same things every week." Here, Doug checked his notepad and rattled off a grocery list. "Oatmeal, bran flakes, bread, milk, soups, instant potatoes, usually a small pack of chicken, some hamburger, and often pork chops, different kinds of cookies, bananas, frozen veggies, and always two six-packs of bottled water."

Fonnie's head quivered when she heard the last item. So maybe Christine's water *was* contaminated, she thought. She'd have to get back to Mike Dickson about that.

"Good job. Anything else?"

"Oh, yes. She bought her gas at Arco."

Fonnie was impressed. "How in the world did you find that out?"

"Guessed. It's across the road from Winn-Dixie, so it seemed logical. Apparently Christine was a creature of habit. Every Friday, after she loaded up on groceries, she filled up with gas. Paid with a credit card. The attendant remembers her because it was always at the same time and usually the same amount. It seems that she only traveled between home and work." Doug paused, gave his audience a knowing smile. "That is until Sunday night."

"What happened Sunday night?" Fonnie asked.

"She came in and filled up again. Since it was so unusual, the attendant remembers asking her where she'd been over the weekend."

Fonnie and everyone else in the room leaned toward Doug. It was Bebe who asked the question, "And what did she tell him?"

"Nothing. He said she seemed so distracted that he

doubted she even heard him. But this is the strangest part. She paid in cash. He said she pulled a twenty out of an envelope—a *fat* envelope." Doug laid down his notepad, crossed his legs and waited for reactions. They weren't long in coming.

Isaac whistled. Patty squeezed Doug's arm. Tyrone said a long, "Wo-o-w."

Jennifer, who had buried herself deep in a wing chair, and who up until now, hadn't made a move or said a word, erupted with excitement. "That's it. Blackmail! Christine found out some dirt about the landfill, and someone gave her money to keep her mouth shut."

Bebe nodded her head. "Then she must have had a change of heart, decided to tell the authorities, and so she had to be killed. If only we could find out what she knew."

Tyrone rubbed his hand across his lips. "Maybe that's what Neil meant by 'we were treading on dangerous ground.' Maybe he's right."

This time Fonnie didn't dispute the possibility. "Let's just go ahead and finish. Jennifer, what do you have to report?"

"Nothing really. I interviewed a neighbor on the opposite side of the road—a widow who lives alone like Christine. They did have a few conversations. She invited Christine to church, but she refused—said she hadn't been to church since her daughter's funeral."

Fonnie bolted upright. "Daughter? I hadn't heard about a daughter. She has two sons, there was no mention of a daughter."

Jennifer looked confused.

"I'm sorry," Fonnie said. "Didn't mean to interrupt. Go ahead, Jennifer. Did she say how long ago the funeral had been?"

"As a matter of fact, she did." Jennifer studied her notes. "Here it is. Christine said, 'I haven't been to church since my daughter's funeral. I guess after nine years the Lord's stopped looking for me.' Then the neighbor—name was Grace D'adria—asked her daughter's age when she died and Christine answered simply, 'Too young.'"

"How sad," Patty said. "But if it happened nine years ago, it can't have anything to do with what's happened now."

Fonnie agreed. "Probably not. Did you have anything else?"

Jennifer shook her head. "I did visit another house on down the road, but the couple there didn't know Christine. They knew about the murder and kept asking me for information, but they didn't have anything to contribute themselves."

"I guess that brings us to you, Tyrone," Fonnie said.

"Actually, I just hung around with Isaac this morning. I thought it might look odd for a young black fellow, alone, to be asking questions about the death of a white woman."

Wise decision, Fonnie thought. "So, Isaac, are you going to fill us in?"

"Well, we made the rounds of the businesses in town, and requested permission to post the memorial flyer. The managers in most places agreed. Some were eager to talk about the terrible crime and others were eager for us to get gone—but nothing particularly suspicious. Then we went to the motel where the Myerson bigwigs were staying and asked to see the CEO. The clerk said he had checked out yesterday, so I asked for Ms. Franklin and the clerk rang her room. I talked to her on the desk phone, told her I'd like to give her a personal invitation to the service. She was rather abrupt and told me to leave it at the desk—that she would pick it up later."

"Sounds good," Fonnie said. "Anything else?"

Isaac shook his head. Tyrone squirmed in his seat, gave a soft teddy-bear smile, and said, "Actually there is something else."

"So out with it," Fonnie said. She was ready for this meeting to end. Her head was beginning to ache, and she needed to go to the bathroom.

"We drove around a while, not knowing exactly what else to do, and then we decided to go out to Christine's house."

"What?" Bebe nearly screamed the question. "You went to the crime scene? Are you both crazy?"

"We didn't violate the crime tape. We simply traversed a narrow lane by the side of the property, got out, and reconnoitered a bit."

"In other words," Fonnie said, "you snooped around." The two young men nodded. "See anything worthwhile?"

"Her car was there," Tyrone said. "At least, I assumed it was Christine's car—an old Honda Civic. The yard looked like it had been kept up nicely—mowed recently and a couple of flower beds that were mulched down for the winter. The house needs painting, but otherwise it looked like quite a nice little bungalow— probably two bedrooms. The only thing that appeared discordant was that the back-porch screen door was unlatched and was being buffeted by the wind."

"And don't forget the chairs on the porch," Isaac said.

"Oh yeah, two yard chairs on the porch were tipped over. Of course, the wind may have done that, but as neat as everything else was on the outside, I doubt if Christine would have left them like that."

Bebe leaned forward. "So what is your explanation?"

Tyrone rubbed his left ear and studied his boots before answering. "Maybe she was dragged from the house, unconscious or dead. The chairs were knocked over in the process and, in his hurry, her assailant didn't bother to pick them up or shut the door."

A sad silence fell over the group. Fonnie imagined the others, like herself, picturing the dreadful scene in their minds.

Bebe broke the silence. She got up, stretched. "I guess we better call it a night. Fonnie has all this on tape. We can go over it later. Thanks again for all your help. We'll see you tomorrow at the service."

Her guests all got up and headed for the door. After a quick trip to the bathroom, Fonnie headed for the computer.

October 20

    So what did our little detective agency learn? That Christine was probably killed at home and her body moved to the landfill. Mike Dickson implied as much when he was here, so that's not really new. What is new is the dead daughter. Does she play a role in all this? And what about the weekend trip Christine made and the wad of money she had? So many questions. So few answers. Maybe tomorrow we'll learn some more. It'll be interesting to see who turns up for the service.

TWELVE

BEBE WAS PLEASED with the way Christine Hauner's memorial service had turned out. It started as a wacky idea, degenerated into a scheming witch hunt, then morphed again into a dignified and touching ceremony. Perhaps twenty people attended, including Lanie Franklin and Ed Whitehall. Many were CATWAG members, who, Bebe suspected, came more out of loyalty to the organization than for Christine.

Fonnie sat near the back between Tyrone and Patty. Her grandson had brought her in earlier, stayed only long enough for a hurried introduction, then muttered that friends were waiting for him at the bowling alley. Bebe assured him one of their group would take Fonnie home. Shortly after Brian left, Bebe was surprised to see Lieutenant Dickson come in, take his time to survey the crowd, and sit down close to Fonnie. Bebe saw them exchange quick smiles just as she headed toward the front to start the service.

"We're here today to honor the memory of Christine Hauner. It seemed fitting for the Citizens Against Toxic Waste At Groverton to host this memorial service for her since she believed in our goals, backed our dream of a safe environment, and did her part in service to our community."

The pastor of Bebe's church gave a brief tribute. He referred to Christine's job of being a home health aide as a life of service to others, a life to be acclaimed, a life to be celebrated. "Even now," he said, "Christine Hauner is standing in the presence of our Lord, awaiting her crown of righteousness." Nothing was said about the terrible way she'd died.

When the opportunity was given for others to speak, two women came forward. One was her neighbor, Grace D'adria. "I didn't know Christine well, but what I did know was that she was a kind, hard-working woman, who loved flowers and Krispy Kreme Donuts. She brought me both last summer when I was laid up with a sprained ankle. I will miss her."

The other woman was Mary Scoggins, her supervisor at the agency. "Christine Hauner was a quiet woman who went about her work with dignity and competence. She served her clients and her community well."

After a short prayer from the minister, Bebe thanked everyone for coming and invited them to stay for coffee and cookies.

Afterwards, Bebe made a point of thanking both Ms. D'adria and Ms. Scoggins for their kind words. While she was chatting with Ms. Scoggins, she was reminded of something she'd forgotten to ask during their earlier visit. "Christine made a remark when she attended one of the CATWAG meetings that has puzzled me. Perhaps you could clarify something for me."

Ms. Scoggins raised her eyebrows and gave a slight shrug. "Clarify what?"

"She said she would like to join our organization, but she couldn't because she was afraid of losing her job.

Does your agency have a policy against employees becoming involved in community issues?"

"Certainly not. I don't know where she got that idea. What employees do on their own time is no business of ours." Ms. Scoggins took a sip of coffee, then added quickly, "As long as it's not illegal or immoral."

"Then you wouldn't have objected if she'd marched in a protest demonstration?"

"Of course not. Not as long as it was a peaceful demonstration and she didn't get arrested for anything."

"I see. Again I thank you for coming and for participating." As Bebe circulated among the guests, she wondered why Christine had thought her job was in jeopardy. Or had it just been a handy excuse?

And come to think of it, where is that sorry excuse of a man, Neil Vincent? Tries to ply me with a jug of wine and then doesn't even have the decency to show up today. Just wait until he calls me again, I'll tell him where he can go with his wine, and believe me, it won't be anywhere near paradise.

Bebe looked up from her ruminations and was dismayed to see Ms. Franklin heading toward the door. But Isaac had taken up a post at the door and was shaking hands, thanking people for coming. His actions delayed Ms. Franklin long enough so Bebe could get to her. She slipped by Isaac and held her own hand out to the Myerson executive. "It was so nice of you to come, Ms. Franklin." Bebe tried desperately to think of some other gracious thing to say, but graciousness didn't come easily to Bebe. She was too accustomed to speaking her mind, and that's what she did now. "Frankly, I'm surprised you'd show your face at the enemy camp. As I'm sure you know, Christine was a staunch supporter of our organization. And her death only makes us more determined to fight on for our cause."

Ms. Franklin looked down from her lofty height, and Bebe tipped her head back until their eyes met. The temperature between them dropped to the freezing point. "I'm here only because I wanted to see for myself what your little charade was all about. And that's exactly what it is, a ploy to get public sympathy. However, you must have forgotten to notify the media. There are no reporters here, so I don't think you'll make the six o'clock news tonight."

The viciousness of Ms. Franklin's remarks stunned Bebe long enough so that the woman was out the door before she could come up with a retort. "Oh yeah," she said to the closing door, "well, I'll see you in court, and there'll be plenty of reporters there."

Bebe turned around and saw Mr. Whitehall heading in her direction. She readied herself for another verbal attack. To her surprise, he was smiling and holding out his hand. His grip was firm and friendly. "A very touching memorial, Mrs. Englehook. Thank you for inviting me. Christine meant a lot to my family. She took such excellent care of Mother."

"Yes," Bebe said, "and thank you for coming."

Before she could say anything else, Mr. Whitehall went on. "I've been wanting to meet Mrs. Beachum. I know she was Christine's other patient. Is she here today?"

"Yes. Yes, she is. Right over there talking to the tall gentleman. Come. I'll introduce you."

Mr. Whitehall followed Bebe across the room. Fonnie and the detective were deep in conversation. Bebe wondered what they were talking about. Was Fonnie telling him about their little investigation and the tape recording? Of course they would share everything they'd learned with the police, but Bebe wanted a little more time to go over the material herself first. Tyrone and Patty had migrated to the door and were chatting with Isaac. Most everybody else had left. Bebe introduced Fonnie to the county commissioner. "So pleased to meet you," he said.

"Likewise."

Before Fonnie could say anything else, Mr. Whitehall turned and shook hands with Detective Dickson. "Good to see you again, detective. Any developments on the case?"

The detective smiled. "We're working on it."

"Good." Mr. Whitehall then turned his attention to Fonnie. "I've been wanting to meet you. Christine spoke so highly of you."

"She did?"

Fonnie looked skeptical. Uh, oh, Bebe thought, is she going to blow this contact like I did with the Franklin gal? But to Bebe's relief, Fonnie turned on her best smile.

"And she told me so much about you, too," Fonnie said. "How kind you were to her. And about your wonderful mother." Fonnie hesitated. "Of course, Christine always had a kind word for everybody. Didn't she?"

"That she did."

At this juncture, Mike Dickson excused himself, told Fonnie and Bebe that he would see them later, shook hands again with Ed Whitehall, and aimed for the door.

Bebe looked around the nearly empty room, glad that her duty as hostess was over. She slipped into a chair just in front of Fonnie and Whitehall, but with her back to them. She wanted to hear what he had to say without seeming to care. Up until now, she had considered him an adversary. He had been the county commissioner who had backed Myerson to the hilt, and refused to listen to any safety issues that CATWAG brought up. She'd tried to meet and talk to him personally, but every time she'd attempted to make an appointment at his office, his secretary would say he was out of town on business or was not available. Now he was sounding like an all right guy. Maybe she'd been mistaken about him.

She unashamedly eavesdropped on their conversation. "Christine was so kind to Mother," he said. "She always went the extra mile, washed her nightgowns with a mild soap by hand because the detergent was too harsh for her delicate skin, always kept her dresser drawers neat. Even brought her little gifts— nothing expensive—just colorful pictures to put on the dresser. Did she ever bring you any pictures?"

"No," Fonnie answered quickly. "She never brought me any pictures. And she never hand-washed my nighties. But," Fonnie smiled as she added, "one day she did tease my hair up quite nicely."

Mr. Whitehall glanced at his watch. "Must be going. I promised my grandson we'd go fishing this afternoon."

The word fishing flashed a neon light on in Bebe's brain. She swung around and faced Ed Whitehall. "Sir, are you aware that if Myerson's proposed landfill is built, it may endanger the fish and wildlife in the Tillent Creek watershed?"

"Mrs. Englehook, I didn't come here today to discuss the landfill. I came as a friend and mourner of dear Christine. Now if you'll excuse me." He turned his back on Bebe and bowed to Fonnie. "So nice to meet you, Mrs. Beachum. Perhaps you'll allow me to call on you sometime."

"Of course, I'd be delighted." She held out her hand for him to shake. Instead he held it gently.

"Or perhaps," he said, "you'd allow me to drive you home now. I'd love to continue our chat."

"But you just said you were going fishing with your grandson."

"Well, yes. But we can do that later. How about it? May I take you home?"

Bebe spun in her chair to face the county commissioner. "No. You can't do that. Fonnie is coming to my house. I have some documents I need to show her—documents that prove the Myerson Corporation has a miserable safety record. I'm sure you'd be interested in them also. You may come along if you wish."

Ed Whitehall gave Bebe a fleeting smile. "Not today, thank you." He turned back to Fonnie. "Perhaps later this evening?"

Again Bebe answered before Fonnie had a chance to say anything. "It may be late when she gets home. I have a lot to show her."

Ed shrugged, gave Fonnie's hand a brief shake, and was gone.

Fonnie turned to Bebe, "What was that all about?"

"I don't trust him. He wanted to get you alone so he could pump you about what you know of CATWAG."

"Don't be ridiculous. You make sure everyone knows what CATWAG thinks." Fonnie brushed her hand over the back of her head to make sure her bald spot wasn't exposed. "But it was rather strange. He's either the nicest gentleman in Groverton—or the biggest liar."

"At any rate," Bebe said, "I do want you and the

others to come to my house for a little bit so we can go over yesterday. Did you bring the tape with you?"

"Sure did." Fonnie patted her purse

"Good. Let me empty the coffee pot, snatch up the rest of the cookies, and we'll head out. But you'll have to ride with one of the others. You and your cane would have trouble getting into my truck."

THIRTEEN

IT WAS AFTER SIX when Tyrone brought Fonnie home. His car was an old Buick, rusty and noisy, but easy to get in and out of. It wasn't completely dark yet since daylight-saving time was still in place. Fonnie dreaded the thought of changing the time back next week. It seemed to make the nights so much longer.

She was surprised Brian wasn't home yet. Fonnie had qualms about entering the empty house alone, but she didn't want to admit it to Tyrone. He walked around the car, opened her door, helped Fonnie out and up the front steps. "Mind if I come in and get a drink of water? Those pretzels of Bebe's had enough salt on them to desiccate a cucumber."

"By all means. Come in. Sit a spell. I have some iced tea in the fridge." She handed Tyrone her key. He unlocked the door and stepped back so she could enter first. She balanced against the door frame as she flipped the light switch. The hallway, bright and cheerful, welcomed them inside.

It wasn't until they made the left turn into the den that she realized something was terribly wrong.

"Whoa, Fonnie, either you've gotten mighty sloppy lately or someone's been messing around in here."

Fonnie stumbled over to the sofa, felt her heart galloping in her chest, stared in dismay at the papers tumbling from the desk, the family pictures torn from the walls and scattered on the floor. Her lips trembled as she stared at Tyrone. "They've already taken my silverware. What else were they after?"

Tyrone picked her phone up from the floor. "We'll let the police figure that out."

TWO UNIFORMED POLICEMEN had been there about ten minutes when Brian bolted into the house. Fonnie stumbled over to him. "Gram! Are you all right? What happened? What's going on here? Why didn't you call me?"

Fonnie tried her best to keep the tears back. She failed. When Brian wrapped his big, strong arms around her, she flooded the front of his jacket. "I don't know what's going on. I don't know what they took. I just know I'm scared."

Brian kept one arm around his grandmother as he shook hands with the other cops. "Wally, Dwayne, what's the story? How'd they get in? Any prints?"

"Too soon to tell," Wally said. "Lab boys on the way. But it looks to me like someone was searching for something."

"Yeah," Dwayne said. "Wonder if he found it."

Fonnie gained control over her emotions, angrily wiped the tears out of her eyes. "You need to call Mike Dickson. This has something to do with Christine Hauner's murder."

Three policemen stared at Fonnie, their eyes puzzled, their mouths partially open. Dwayne broke the silence. "You knew the murdered woman?"

"She worked for me. She had incriminating evidence against somebody. She blackmailed him or her. Then she changed her mind and was killed. But she hid the evidence. That's what they were after. They think she hid it here. It's all very clear now."

Brian walked Fonnie over to the sofa and sat down with her. He placed his hands on his grandmother's shoulders. "It's not clear at all. You know nothing of the kind. You're imagining all this."

Tyrone stepped forward from where he'd been standing in the far corner. "She may be right. It makes sense."

Brian whirled around, glowered at the boy. "And who in the world are you?"

"Oh," Fonnie gasped. "I'd forgotten you two hadn't met. This is Tyrone Riggs, Keisha's brother. He's cleaning up the yard for me. He was kind enough to give me a ride home from the memorial service."

Brian rose, went over and stood toe to toe with the brown hunk. "It doesn't look to me like you've done much yard cleaning. And the memorial service has been over for hours. I drove by there about four and the place was empty."

Tyrone took a step back. "Yes sir, you're right. I haven't done much yard work yet, but I plan to this week. And after the service a bunch of us went over to Bebe's—for refreshments. And then I brought Mrs. Beachum home."

"And what do you know about Christine?"

Before Tyrone could answer, Wally touched Brian on the shoulder. His voice was low, but Fonnie could hear the words. "You just live here. Dwayne and I are the investigating officers. And I think your grandmother is right. We need to call Lieutenant Dickson."

Mike arrived in a few minutes. He grinned at Fonnie. "Didn't expect to see you again so soon."

"Me either. Although I did intend to call you tomorrow and fill you in."

The detective rubbed his hand over his darkening chin. "To tell me something you should have told me this afternoon—and didn't?"

"Yes. But Bebe and I wanted to think about it a little more."

"So you and Mrs. Englehook are in cahoots. I thought there was something fishy about that memorial service."

"Fishy? What's fishy?" Brian's head pivoted from the detective to his grandmother and back again. "Will someone tell me what's going on here?"

Fonnie gave them both a weak smile. "Mike, have you met my grandson?"

"Yes, I've met Officer Hendley. But it seems like you've been keeping things from both of us."

Brian gave Mike a lopsided grin. "Gram has a tendency to go off on her own when she gets some wild idea."

"So I've noticed." Mike looked over at the lab crew and the other officers. "Tell you what—let me find out what we know so far and then the three of us will have a little chat."

"Can you make that four of us?" Fonnie asked. "Tyrone should be in on it too."

"Actually," Tyrone said, "I should be getting home. Pop always expects me to attend the Sunday evening service. I don't know anything more than what's on the tape."

"Tape?" Mike's eyebrows shot up.

"Tape?" Brian echoed. "What tape?"

"I'll explain in a little bit. It's all right then for Tyrone to leave?"

"Sure." Mike waved permission for the boy to go.

"I'll contact you later if I need to." As Tyrone scooted out the door, the detective turned to Brian. "While I'm talking to the lab boys, you can find us a place to meet where we won't be in their way."

Brian led Dickson and Fonnie to the library. The door opened inward, hiding the desk and the TV at the far right of the room. If someone just glanced through the door, all he would see would be some cardboard boxes to the left and shelves of old books in front. "I don't think the intruder came in here," Brian said. "None of my papers seem to be disturbed." He carried in the captain's chair from the dining room for Fonnie, a straight chair for himself, and motioned the lieutenant to the desk chair. "This used to be a store room, and if our visitor looked in, he may have decided it wasn't worth searching, or he ran out of time."

"And what is it used for now?"

"Studying. I have a VCR and DVD player for my training tapes, my books and notes on the desk. That's about it. Nothing that would interest anyone else. But," Brian added, "I used a paper towel to open the door just in case there were prints on the knob."

Fonnie beamed at her grandson. Here stood the makings of a great cop, maybe someday a top detective like Mike.

Mike grunted. "Good. Now let's get to this tape of yours, Fonnie."

Fonnie shook her head. "You first."

Brian recoiled in his chair. "Gram, you can't talk to the lieutenant that way."

Mike laughed. "I suspect your grandmother is accustomed to talking any way she likes to anybody. So, what do you want to find out from me first?"

"How did our friend get in? Brian had deadbolt locks installed on both the front and back doors."

"Right, but there are plenty of ground floor windows with locks as old as the house. The window from the back porch to the utility area was open. Probably easy enough to slide a knife up through the crack, open the lock, and then slide up the window."

"Oh Lord," Brian whispered. "I didn't even think about the windows." He reached over and patted Fonnie's arm. "Don't you worry. I'll do something with them—put bars up if I have to. No one is going to break in here again."

Mike went on as if Brian hadn't said anything. "The lab boys are doubtful about prints. We'll get the family prints to compare and then any of friends you've had in lately, but the intruder probably wore gloves. The main thing we need to do is to find out what he was searching for. And then decide if it has any connection to the murder." He picked up his pen, positioned it over his notepad, turned to Fonnie. "And that's where you come in."

Fonnie started by telling the two men about her and Bebe's idea for the memorial service and their plan for a discreet investigation. Then she pulled out the tape recorder that she had slipped from her purse into the pocket of her jacket. "I recorded our meeting so you can hear the reports in their own words. And believe me, when this tape is finished, you'll want to put all of us on your payroll."

Mike smiled. Brian looked like he needed some extra-strength antacid. Fonnie knew he was embarrassed by her playing detective in front of the real detective from his department. Well, that was tough. He'd just have to get used to it.

She started the tape. It began with a loud tap and Fonnie's voice asking, "Can we get started now?" Fonnie had listened to the tape earlier that day with Bebe and the others, but she was beginning to love the sound of her own voice, and she sat back to enjoy the encore.

They were only a few seconds into the tape when Mike motioned her to hand the recorder to him. She did so and he immediately rewound a short section. Bebe's voice was quoting Neil Vincent saying that "we were treading on dangerous ground" and "that the less we knew, the better."

Mike turned off the machine. "What do you think he meant by that?"

Fonnie shrugged. Brian supplied his own answer. "I think this Vincent fellow knows more than he's letting on. He knew Christine. He identified the body. He may know why she was killed."

"We'll get back to him." Mike started the tape rolling again. He made no comment about Bebe's visit to Ms. Scoggins nor to the Whitehall home. Patty's report on the neighbors seemed to evoke little interest. Doug's story about Christine's shopping habits elicited only a faint "Umm."

But Fonnie motioned to him, and Mike stopped the tape. "What?"

"The water. Remember I told you Christine was afraid to drink my tap water, and here she is buying bottled water every week. Don't you find that peculiar?"

"Gram, lots of people buy bottled water to drink," Brian said.

"Not unsophisticated people like Christine—who only makes a little over minimum wage—who has her own well water." Fonnie pointed her right index finger at the detective. "You said you were going to have her water tested."

"I did. Pure as a virgin stream."

"But she was afraid to drink it. Why?"

"I haven't quite figured that out yet." His thumb rested on the play button. "Can we continue?"

Fonnie nodded. She knew the bombshell was coming up next and waited for Mike's reaction. When Doug mentioned Christine filling her car up with gas on Sunday night, and how the attendant said this was very unusual, Mike stopped the tape again.

"So," Fonnie said, "the plot thickens. What mysterious trip did Christine make?"

"Nothing mysterious about it," Mike replied. "She went to visit her daughter's grave in Emmetsville, Virginia."

"You know about the trip?" Fonnie's face fell like a half-baked souffle. "You know about the dead daughter?"

"I'm a detective. Remember?"

"And a very good one," Fonnie said.

"I like to think so."

"See, Gram," Brian said. "The lieutenant and the police don't need your help to solve this case. That's what I've been telling you."

"Yeah, yeah. Then you know about the money too." It was a statement, not a question.

But to Fonnie's surprise and delight, Mike responded with his own question, "What money?"

"Oh," she said, sitting up straighter. "You don't know about the fat money envelope that Christine was carrying." Mike shook his head. "So listen up," Fonnie said, "then tell me you don't need my help. Start the tape." Mike did as he was told.

Doug's excited voice went on, "she pulled a twenty out

of an envelope—a *fat* envelope." Mike pushed the stop button, rewound a little and played it again, "*fat* envelope."

Brian rolled his eyes. "Is that all? It was probably just the rest of her pay that she hadn't gotten around to putting in her billfold." He looked over at Mike. "What do you think?"

"I think I would like a better definition of *fat*. I'll stop at Arco and fill up with gas on my way home. Hopefully the same attendant will be on duty." Mike smiled at Fonnie. "What conclusion did you and your cohorts come to about the money?"

"Push the switch and you'll hear exactly what we concluded." Mike did that and heard about the blackmail theory, and about Christine's possible change of heart.

"Could be," he murmured. "Could be."

The trio continued to listen carefully while Jennifer spoke of the dead daughter. Fonnie signaled for Mike to stop the tape. "You said Christine visited her daughter's grave on the very Sunday she was killed. Surely the two events are linked."

"Maybe. Maybe not. In interviewing an old friend of Christine's who happens to live next door to the cemetery, I found out Christine always visited her daughter close to the anniversary of her death."

"Which was Sunday?" Brian said.

"Yes. However, there was one unusual thing about the trip."

"And that was?" Fonnie asked.

"This friend saw Christine in the cemetery and expected her to come over for a visit as she had done every other year, but that day Christine got in her car and drove away. Didn't even stop in to say hello. Apparently didn't stop to see anybody."

Fonnie frowned. "Not even her boys? Don't they live near there?"

"They live a few miles away, but they hadn't seen their mother in nearly four years. Some kind of family rift occurred that I haven't gotten to the bottom of yet. However, according to the sheriff there, they gave her a nice funeral. She's buried next to the girl."

"When was the funeral?" Fonnie asked.

"Friday. The medical examiner here released the body on Thursday." Before Fonnie could ask anything else, Mike quickly added, "And I'm not going to tell you anything about his report."

"You don't have to. Bebe said that Neil said she'd been struck on her head." Fonnie sighed. "Poor Christine." She took off her glasses and rubbed her eyes. She was getting another headache. They seemed to be coming more often lately. Little wonder. Probably her blood pressure was sky high. In all of the excitement, she probably forgot to take her pills this morning. She wondered when this nightmare would end, and when her life could get back to normal.

"Can we move on?" Mike had already pushed the play button when Fonnie stopped him. He quickly turned the machine back off.

"One more thing. How old was the daughter and what did she die of?"

Mike groaned as if he too was getting a headache. "Nine. Cancer. A malignant brain tumor to be exact."

Brian leaned forward. "What would cause a brain tumor in a nine-year-old?"

"Doctors say it happens. They can't usually pinpoint a cause." The detective hesitated, looked at Fonnie, started the tape. The three sat in silence while Isaac told his story. It wasn't until Tyrone spoke of going to Christine's house to look around the yard that Brian gave a choking sound and Mike leaned back in his chair and studied the ceiling. At the end of the tape, Mike's only comment was, "It's a good thing that boy is going to church tonight."

FOURTEEN

WALLY STUCK HIS HEAD in the library. "Sir, if you're finished with Mrs. Beachum, I'd like her and Brian to check around again to see if anything is missing."

"Fine. I'm getting ready to go."

"But you can't go yet," Fonnie said. "I want to ask you some more questions."

Brian buried his face in his hands and groaned like a sick puppy. The lieutenant tried to smile, but didn't quite succeed. "Not now. I have some more calls to make. Perhaps I can get back to you tomorrow."

Fonnie pretended not to realize she was being dismissed. "Good. Come for lunch. I'll order something in and we can tie up some loose ends." She grabbed her cane and toddled out of the room. "Now Wally, what was it you wanted?"

Although the house looked as if a mini-twister had ripped through it, Fonnie and Brian concluded that nothing had been stolen. The desk was ransacked, the kitchen drawers were searched, pictures and knick-knacks were turned over, the sofa cushions were upended, the linen closet and dresser drawers mauled over, but nothing seemed to be missing.

When she and Brian were finally alone, Fonnie collapsed on the den sofa. Her brain, her sense of security, her sense of humor, her brave facade, all caved in on themselves. She was drained of emotion, of thoughts. She just wanted to curl up under her afghan and feel safe again.

"Can I get you anything?" Brian's face was contorted with concern.

Fonnie wanted to reassure him that she was fine, but she couldn't quite come out with the lie. "A cup of tea would be nice." She managed a smile. "And then you can tip my world back right side up."

He sat down beside her. "Maybe Mom is right. Maybe you should sell the house, move into a nice senior apartment. This neighborhood really isn't safe anymore, with the video store and gas stations just a block away. Dwayne thinks whoever broke in probably parked at a store and walked down here so his car wouldn't be seen."

"Makes sense. And it could happen again. I guess maybe you'd better see about putting up those window bars you talked about."

Later as she sipped her tea and munched the tuna sandwich Brian had brought her, Fonnie began to perk up. Maybe I was just hungry, she thought. Those chips and cookies at Bebe's really didn't constitute dinner. At the thought of Bebe, Fonnie asked Brian to hand her the phone and her rolodex. "I've got to warn Bebe about what's going on."

Brian obediently brought them, but voiced his objection. "This has nothing to do with Bebe. She denied even speaking with Christine." Brian went on even as Fonnie dialed the number. "You've convinced me someone was looking for something connected with Christine—maybe something she gave you to keep for her—or something she hid here—perhaps whatever she was using for blackmail. What does Bebe have to do with that?"

Fonnie held up her hand to stop his flow of words. "Bebe," she began, "do you have good locks on all your windows?"

Fonnie went into great detail about what had happened and then listened as Bebe insisted there was absolutely no reason for anybody to break into her house. "True," Fonnie said. "You know and I know Christine didn't give you anything, but my uninvited guest may think differently. Or he may think I gave you something to hide, something incriminating Christine may have given me." Fonnie took a deep breath after that mouthful of words. "And furthermore, since you gave the memorial service, he's bound to think you and Christine were close friends. And as buddies, she may have shared secrets with you." Fonnie paused to let the message soak into her friend's head. "Just be careful. That's all I'm asking. Please be careful."

After she hung up, Brian pulled the desk chair closer to the sofa. "Did you?"

"Did I what?"

"Did you give Bebe anything that belonged to Christine? Or tell her anything that you haven't told the police?"

"Of course not. In the first place, Christine never gave me anything. Ed said that she gave his mother some pictures, but she never gave me any."

"Ed?"

"Ed Whitehall. His mother was Christine's other client. But then you know that. And the police have already questioned everybody there." Fonnie swallowed the last dregs of her tea, set the cup down. She looked hard at her grandson. "Tell me the truth. Do you think our intruder found what he was looking for—or will he be back?"

"I don't think he found it. I think he may have heard

you and Tyrone pull up and scooted out the way he came in. When I was checking upstairs, I could tell that Mom's old bedroom had been only partially ransacked. Since the room looks out over the driveway, he could have seen you coming in."

Fonnie pondered a moment. "In that case, we only missed him by a couple of minutes—the time it took me to get out of the car and up the steps."

"Seems like. But he may not risk coming back. Wally said he was going to request extra patrol cars for the neighborhood. They'll be driving by at various times and checking for anything suspicious."

"We keep saying, 'he'," Fonnie said, "but it could have been a woman."

"Sure. Any suspects in mind? Male or female?"

"Nary a one."

BEBE HUNG UP the phone with Fonnie's warning swirling in her head. Be careful. She gave an involuntary shudder. It was the same warning her college son had given her a few minutes earlier. He'd made his usual weekly call, gave her a play-by-play description of last night's football game, updated her on his latest girlfriend, and then asked about her day. She very foolishly told him.

"Be careful, Mom," he said. "Those are some really big wheels you're aggravating. We're talking corporate profits here, and some corporations will let nothing and no one stand in the way of their profits."

She pooh-poohed his concern, assured him there was nothing to worry about. "Besides I have some big wheels on my side. The Environmental Defense League is not to be taken lightly. When we get to court, Myerson will see he has more to contend with than just little ole me."

Still, his words worried her, and now Fonnie had come along with the same message. Surely no one would want to break into her house. There would be no reason for it. All the information she had about the Myerson Corporation was in public documents. All she had done was to sift through the legalese and point out the company's safety problems.

She certainly knew nothing about Christine's controversy with Myerson. And therein lay the dilemma. Fonnie was probably right about people assuming she had been good friends with Christine. And good friends often share secrets.

Bebe wandered through her house, checking on doors and windows, closing blinds, and telling herself that the memorial service had been a dumb idea.

She was halfway through her grapefruit the next morning when she had another idea. Since someone might think she knew Christine's secrets, it was probably in her best interest to find out what those secrets were. She dialed Fonnie's number.

"How about driving up to Emmetsville, Virginia with me today? It's not far over the state line. And before you ask me why, I'll tell you why. That's where Christine hailed from and where she's buried. It was in her obituary. We need to find out what the rift was in Christine's family. We need to know more about her daughter's death, and to find out if Christine had any prior contact or run-in with the Myerson Corporation."

Bebe listened to Fonnie's objections and answered all of them. "So, call Dickson and postpone your lunch date, not that he was going to come anyway, and call Keisha, tell her to take the day off. I know it would be hard for you to get into my truck, so I'm borrowing a friend's Camry. It's low, comfortable, and most important, fast. I promise we'll stop every hour so you can get out and stretch your rickety old joints. But I need you. People are more apt to open up to a sweet old lady like yourself than to a young— well, young in comparison, nosy person like myself. I'll run to the bookstore and put a sign up saying I'm closed for remodeling. There's never much business on Mondays."

When Fonnie finally agreed to go, Bebe added, "And there's no need to tell Brian where we're going. Just leave him a note saying you're spending the day with me doing research about the landfill. I promise I'll get you home before midnight." Bebe laughed as Fonnie sputtered something about getting home before dark.

Bebe dressed in blue jeans and a sweat shirt, and grabbed a hooded parka. The day was sunny, but cool. And the higher elevations were always cooler. She hurried through her arrangements, packed some snacks and filled a thermos with coffee just in case there was a dearth of open restaurants. Many tourist places closed their doors at the first frost.

She went out, hoisted herself into her truck, headed to the bookstore to post the Closed notice and then planned to swing by and trade cars with Betty. As she exited her drive, she checked the rear-view mirror and noticed a black car across the street parked in front of the Johnson place. It was close to nine and the Johnsons both left for work much earlier. She craned around to see if anybody sat in the car. She wasn't sure. It might be a man, or it might be she was just seeing a shadow from a nearby spruce tree. Bebe scolded herself for being nervous. No one was going to break into her house. If anyone did, he wouldn't find anything worth taking.

FONNIE LOOKED WORRIED when she opened the door. "I thought you'd be excited about doing some more investigation," Bebe said. "And here you are, looking like you're headed for a dentist appointment."

"A dentist drill might be preferable to the lecture I'm going to get from Brian when I get home. He called Amy last night, told her about the break-in. He suggested I go up there and stay with her until all this is settled."

"And what did your daughter say?"

"I'm not sure, but it upset Brian. It seems that she and her boyfriend are going to New York for a few days. Brian interpreted that to mean she couldn't be bothered with me. I'm sure that's not what she meant. Besides, I tried to tell him I didn't want to go anywhere."

"Except with me today."

Fonnie's face relented and she gave Bebe a smile. "Yes, except with you. But, unfortunately, I don't think Brian will understand."

"Suppose I leave my cell phone number for him. That should soothe some of his ruffled feathers. And if it looks like we're going to be late getting back, you can call him. All right?"

"All right. Let's go."

They rode in silence going out of town, through open country, past scattered farm houses, signs pointing to 220 North. Finally Fonnie spoke up. "You seem to know where you're going."

"Yep. Got it all planned out. First, we go to the cemetery where we plant flowers on Christine's and her daughter's graves. My friend, Betty, runs a greenhouse and I got some bronze and yellow chrysanthemums from her. They're in the trunk, along with trowels and water. You told me last night that Dickson mentioned a friend of Christine's who lived next to the cemetery. Therefore she'll probably observe our little labor of love and it should convince her that we're Christine's friends also. We'll introduce ourselves and then squeeze her for information about Christine's previous life and family."

"Devious. I like the way your mind works."

"And then we'll find the ex-husband and the sons and grill them. I read Christine's obit online in her hometown newspaper, and it gave the boys' names. Then I found their addresses."

"I'm impressed. I must learn more about searching for stuff on the internet. But I detect one little flaw in your plans."

"What's that?"

"I think most people will be working. It's unlikely we'll find anyone at home."

"I thought about that," Bebe said. "In which case, we'll just widen our circle—talk to anyone we can find." She nodded her head at the steering wheel. "We'll find out something. I have a good feeling about today."

"I hope you're right."

FIFTEEN

THE CLOSER THEY CAME to the Virginia state line, the barer the trees became. What few leaves still clung to the branches were just waiting for the next strong breeze to whisk them to the ground. "Too bad we couldn't have come a couple of weeks ago," Fonnie said. "The colors would have been at their peak." She stared out the window at the rolling hills, at the Hereford cattle in the pastures searching for patches of green the frost might have missed. "Harrison and I used to drive up the Parkway every year for the fall foliage." Her body relaxed as she thought of past autumns, past beauty, past love. "I remember one year, the colors were especially spectacular. The fiery reds, the glowing yellows, the brilliant oranges. We stopped into a coffee shop and I remarked about the beautiful colors to the waitress. And she replied, 'Oh really, I haven't had time to notice.' Imagine, living in the midst of such God-given beauty and not taking time to notice."

Bebe took her eyes off the road long enough to give Fonnie an understanding smile. "I know what you mean. But I guess we're all guilty of it at times."

Fonnie nodded. "Like not seeing the beauty in a person until they're gone."

"You're not going maudlin on me, are you?" Bebe asked as she slowed down for an approaching curve.

"Me? Maudlin? Don't be ridiculous."

They found the cemetery easily, located behind a small brick Baptist church. It was well kept, surrounded by an iron picket fence. Bebe parked the car and helped Fonnie out. Fonnie walked around slowly, getting the kinks out of her joints and reading the inscriptions. Some of the markers dated back over a hundred years. Fonnie liked old cemeteries. They offered individuality and a testimony of faith—faith passed down through generations.

Bebe showed no interest in the old graves as she glanced around the small cemetery. "I see a fresh grave there near the back. That must be Christine's. I'm going to move the car closer."

Fonnie declined a ride and took her time shuffling past the stone monuments and the faded bouquets of plastic flowers. By the time she reached Christine's grave, Bebe was nearly finished planting the chrysanthemums. Bronze-colored blossoms decorated the freshly dug grave while perky gold flowers nestled in the green blanket that covered Alice Marie Hauner's resting place. Fonnie bowed her head and mourned for both the mother and the daughter. Were they separate tragedies? Or was there an evil thread connecting the two? Maybe today, Fonnie thought, we'll find some answers.

Bebe patted the last bit of dirt around the plants, stood up and stretched. "They won't live long with winter coming, but it's the thought that counts." She glanced over at the gray-shingled bungalow to their left, just over the cemetery fence. "We're being watched."

Fonnie's gaze followed the fence around to the backyard of the neighboring house. She pushed her glasses up and could make out a figure in the shadows of the porch. "Maybe that's Christine's friend. Do you think she would be kind enough to give two tired, thirsty mourners a glass of cold water?"

"No harm in asking," Bebe said as she took off her gardening gloves. Fonnie climbed in the car while Bebe loaded her tools and empty pots in the trunk. They drove slowly out of the cemetery, hooked a right, and followed the road to a dirt driveway.

When they turned into the drive, Fonnie noted the woman on the porch coming down the steps to watch their approach.

After introductions and an explanation of their cemetery visit, the woman invited them up to the porch. "Come and sit a spell. I'll bring you a glass of tea. No need for you to hurry away."

The neighbor's name was Sybil Welch. She was fiftyish, friendly, and voluble. "I'm so glad to meet some friends of Christine. You know I worried about her when she moved away."

"Worried?" Fonnie asked. "Why?"

"Because it was hard for her to make friends. Christine wasn't a very outgoing person. We worked together for years before we really became friends and started visiting back and forth."

Bebe sipped her iced tea. "You worked with her?"

"Yes. We were both nurse assistants on the maternity floor. We were pretty busy back then. Now most of the women go to larger towns to have their babies. In fact, I don't think any of the old doctors around here even deliver babies anymore. I had to quit work. Bad back, you know. But ten, fifteen years ago our little hospital was really bustling. And I loved it. Then came the questions."

Bebe slowly set her glass down. "Questions?"

Sybil nodded. "About the babies. About why so many were stillborn or died soon after birth. And about the defects."

Fonnie and Bebe gaped at each other. Fonnie leaned closer to their hostess. "How tragic. I'm a nurse and I worked in the delivery room of a small hospital for years. I know how terrible it is when a baby dies, or is born with a deformity. I guess it hurt you and Christine and the other staff members pretty badly."

"It certainly did. Of course, at first the doctors thought it was just one of those things, a streak of bad luck. But when the cases started piling up the rumors started. Some blamed the noise from the new airport, some thought it was a poison in the air, in the water, in the hospital. It wasn't long before the place was crawling with people from state agencies." Sybil refilled their glasses. "Would you like some cookies? Got some gingersnaps that will really tickle your tongue."

Both Bebe and Fonnie shook their heads. Fonnie wanted to shout, *So what did they find?* Instead she asked quietly, "Did they find the cause?"

"Who knows? Depends on who you ask. The state health department said it was some leakage from the dump that got into the water. The landfill company denied it, said it was air pollution from the factories on the other side of the river. The state fined both of them, ordered the dump to clean up and the factories to build better filters."

Bebe cleared her throat. "What was the name of the landfill company?"

Fonnie held her breath for the answer.

"Let's see now. I should remember. It was in all the papers at the time. They still run the place, but I guess it's okay now. Hadn't heard anything lately. What *is* their name?"

Sybil paused so long, Fonnie decided to help her out. "I seem to remember Christine mentioning it to me once," Fonnie said. "Was it Myerson?"

"That's it! Myerson. I remember now. It was on TV and everything. The president of the company even came here and talked to us. They had a big meeting at the courthouse. He was such a nice gentleman. He assured us that there was absolutely no leakage from his landfill, but in a show of good faith, he agreed to install a new waterproof lining." Sybil smiled at the memory. "Such a nice man." Sybil's smile faded as apparently another memory slipped into place. "But that was the same time when Alice was real sick."

"Christine's daughter?" Fonnie asked.

"Yes. She was the joy of Christine's life. Oh, she loved her boys too, but the sun rose and set on Alice. When Christine heard about the leakage from the dump, there was no reasoning with her."

"What do you mean, 'reasoning'?" Bebe said.

Sybil shrugged. "No one could talk any sense into her. She swore that Myerson had poisoned her daughter, that Alice got cancer from drinking the water. She even went up to the stage after the meeting and called the company officials murderers."

Fonnie and Bebe looked at each other. Bebe found her voice first. "You mean, she confronted Mr. Myerson?"

"No. He'd already left. But she was yelling at some other people from the company. I went up and finally got her away from there."

"Did you see who the other people were?" Fonnie asked.

Sybil shook her head. "I wasn't paying any attention to them. I just wanted to get Christine out."

Fonnie's mind whirled around. Wait until Mike hears this, she thought. Could Lanie Franklin have been the object of Christine's wrath?

Sybil went on, "Of course, that's what led to the divorce."

"How was that?" Bebe said.

"Because Ralph, that was Christine's husband, worked for Myerson. He drove a bulldozer at the dump. You know, pushing things around, burying it. Christine insisted he quit and Ralph refused. The boys sided with their dad. The oldest one, Junior, even got a job there himself when he graduated from high school. I didn't blame them. Jobs around here weren't plentiful back then—still aren't. Men have to take what work they can find. But Christine didn't see it that way. She accused them of siding with Alice's murderer. It got to be more than poor Ralph could take, and he walked out. Junior went with him."

Fonnie understood why Christine needed someone to blame for Alice's death. She knew from her hospital experience that when a child died it was just too painful to say it was God's will or that it was meant to be. The parents often wanted someone to blame.

"So," Fonnie asked, "that's when Christine moved to North Carolina?"

"Not right then. She wanted to, but Mark, the younger boy, wanted to stay here, so Christine stayed until he graduated. Then I guess she couldn't take it any longer. She told me she had to get away from the memories." Sybil shook her head. "As if moving a hundred miles or so would ease the pain."

Fonnie thanked Sybil for her hospitality and for being such a good friend to Christine. "I know she'll rest easy now that she's next to Alice and with you watching over them."

They shook hands and Sybil's voice followed them down the steps. "I'm glad you stopped in. Why didn't the gentleman come in too? Wasn't he thirsty?"

Bebe jerked her head up. "What gentleman?"

"Why, the one in the black car that followed you. He drove up on the other side of the cemetery while you were planting the flowers. I thought he must be with you."

"No," Bebe said. "He wasn't with us. He must have been visiting another grave."

"Yes," said Sybil, "I guess so."

SIXTEEN

"THREE BIRDS WITH one stone." Fonnie got in on the passenger side, leaned her cane against the dashboard, grinned. "Amazing detective work if I do say so myself." Bebe started the car and backed out of the narrow driveway. She turned to her companion as she pointed the car toward the blacktop road that led back to the cemetery. "What three birds?"

"The three objectives you said we had for this trip. One—finding out what caused the rift in Christine's family. Two—learning more about her daughter's death. And three—discovering her prior contact with Myerson. Sybil, bless her heart, gave us the answers to all of them."

"That she did, plus a lot more. We know why Christine opposed our landfill, why she bought bottled water, why she moved away."

Fonnie nodded. "What we don't know is who she tried to blackmail and why she changed her mind. When we find that out, we'll know who killed her."

"Wait a minute. Remember, the blackmail angle is only supposition. We have no proof that's where her wad of money came from and we're only guessing she changed her mind and tried to return the money."

"True. But the money wasn't found on her or in her house. If it had been, Mike wouldn't have been so surprised when he learned about the money in the envelope."

"That makes sense." They passed the entrance to the cemetery and Bebe slowed down at the county road that ran north and south. "So which way now? Do we try to hunt down the ex-husband and the sons or some old neighbors? Or do we head back home and lay our information in Dickson's lap?"

There was no hesitation in Fonnie's answer. "We find a restaurant with a clean restroom. When I've emptied my bladder and filled my stomach, we can decide on the next move."

"Sounds good to me. Emmetsville is right ahead. And I've got a hankering for some good Virginia ham and black-eyed peas."

"With a little corn bread thrown in," Fonnie added.

THE WAITRESS WAS YOUNG, bored, and tight-lipped. After the meal, Bebe tried to get some information out of her. She denied knowing any Hauners, and she hadn't heard that one of the town's former residents had been murdered. "Might have been something about it in the paper, but I never read the paper, 'cept for movie times." She refilled their iced tea glasses, shifted the gum in her mouth, and asked without enthusiasm if they wanted anything else. Fonnie could tell the girl wanted a negative answer. She and Bebe both shook their heads.

Bebe spoke what Fonnie was thinking. "Might as well head back. I doubt we'll learn anything more around here."

They'd gone a couple of miles when Fonnie said, "It's funny how cars are a lot like horses."

"Okay, I'll play along," Bebe said. "How are cars like horses?"

"They always go faster when they're headed home."

"Are you implying I'm driving too fast?"

"Well, you did take that last curve on two wheels. There's a reason, you know, why the highway department puts up those pretty yellow caution signs."

"You did say you wanted to get home before dark."

"Yes. But did I forget to mention I wanted to get there in one piece?"

"Picky. Picky." Bebe slid her foot over to the brake pedal and gentled the car down to thirty-five. "Now if that guy on my tail would just pass me, we could enjoy the scenery."

Fonnie turned her head so she could see the car behind them. "You're not kidding about him on your tail. Hasn't he ever heard of a safe following distance?"

"Apparently not. Should I pull over and you can explain it to him?"

Fonnie shifted her hips so she could get a better view of the car and the driver. Her voice quivered a little when she spoke again. "Bebe, it's a man in a black car."

"So?"

"Sybil said a man in a black car followed us into the cemetery."

Bebe tilted her head to look in the mirror again. "You know, I think that car was outside the restaurant too. I noticed a black Honda as we came out. I didn't see the driver, though."

"There's a straight stretch of road ahead. Slow down more and he'll have to pass."

Bebe tapped the brakes. The speed indicator needle dipped to thirty, to twenty-five. The car behind slowed down to a crawl. Bebe craned her neck for a closer look. "Fonnie," she whispered, "I don't like telling you this, but I think that's the same car that was across the street from my house when I left this morning. Someone has been following us all day."

A shiver of fear trembled over Fonnie's body. "But why?"

"Because we're getting close to finding Christine's murderer. That has to be it. I'm going to make a sudden stop and when I do, you try to get a good look, see if he looks at all familiar."

Before Fonnie had a chance to protest, Bebe jammed the brake pedal, the Camry jerked and swayed. The driver of the car behind reacted quickly, coming to a sudden stop. And then just as quickly, he backed up and then shot forward. His front bumper collided with the Camry's back bumper jarring Fonnie's teeth and her psyche. "Damn," she cried out. "Let's get the hell out of here!"

"Right." Bebe floored the gas pedal. As the Camry shot forward, she turned her head slightly toward Fonnie. "But I'm shocked at your flowery language."

Tires squealed, purses levitated, Fonnie's cane flew back and hit her knees. "You'll hear a lot worse if that guy catches up with us."

The Camry ate up the straight stretch of road in about two nanoseconds and straddled the double yellow lines around the next two sharp curves. The rolling hills by the side of the road blocked Fonnie's view of the black car, but she sensed it wasn't far behind.

Bebe kept her eyes on the road. "Did you get a good look at him?"

"Not too good, but nothing about him looked familiar."

"Probably a hired hood. Dale Myerson would hardly do his own dirty work."

Fonnie clung to the door handle as Bebe careened

around another S curve. "So you think Myerson is behind all this?"

"I'd bet my last—" A screeching horn from a red convertible fast approaching them drowned out the rest of Bebe's sentence.

Fonnie shuddered, gasped, slumped down in her seat. Bebe screamed as she skidded the car close to the edge of the road. The crunch of gravel jerked Fonnie's eyes to the window. She could see the roof of a mobile home directly below. She motioned frantically for Bebe to twist the steering wheel to the left. Bebe swerved the car back onto the roadway just as a flash of red appeared in front of them.

The red oncoming car and the blue Camry almost traded paint as both drivers claimed the road as their own. By some miracle, the cars made it around the curve without colliding.

Fonnie gulped in a ragged breath of mountain air as the convertible whizzed by. The young man at the wheel loosened his grip just long enough to give them the finger. "No more talk," Fonnie commanded. "You drive. I'll pray."

Fonnie twisted around in her seat to see if the convertible had safely made it around the next curve. It had, but so had the black Honda. It came up behind them like a predatory monster.

The distance between the two cars was several yards— then feet—then inches. Fonnie screamed. "He's going to ram us!"

The sound of the thud was muted by Bebe's shriek and Fonnie's howl. In those few moments that the Camry was airborne, Fonnie felt that both her stomach and her heart doing flip-flops.

Their car slammed to a stop and came to rest on a crushed guardrail. It teetered there like a playground see-saw. Fonnie was glued to the passenger door, and she saw Bebe's right hip jammed into the gear shift.

The black car swirled around them, tossing gravel in its wake. Fonnie looked up in time to see a red and blue North Carolina license plate vanish around the next curve.

Silence followed the Honda's disappearance. Bebe's hands were cemented to the steering wheel, her breaths came in short jerks.

Fonnie was afraid to move. She rolled her head slightly to the right. Her side of the car seemed to be hanging in midair hovering over a chasm of sharp rocks.

Maybe it wasn't as bad as it looked, Fonnie thought. Maybe the drop wasn't very far.

Bebe reached over, switched off the motor, turned her head to Fonnie. "Reckon the car will tip over if we wiggle?"

Fonnie nodded. "Looks like."

"I'm sorry I got you into this mess."

Fonnie tried to smile. "We'll go into that later."

"There's going to be a later?"

Fonnie sat up straight, careful not to disturb the car's equilibrium. "That depends. How are you at slithering?"

"Pardon me?"

"Making like a snake. Slide over to your door without a quiver or a vibration. While you're doing that, I'll squirm over to your seat. Maybe with both our weights on that side we can keep the car from going over."

"Too bad we're both petite. This is the first time in my life I've wished I weighed two hundred pounds."

Fonnie was trying her best to keep her terror in check and she figured Bebe was doing the same. Nothing like a little gallows humor to ease the tension. "No way," Fonnie said. "There would just be more of you to splatter when this buggy tumbles over."

Bebe shuddered. "Thanks a lot for that image. So I guess I have to get my tiny hiney in gear and start slithering."

Bebe started slithering and sliding on her uphill seat until her fingers rested on the door handle. Fonnie twisted her neck around so she could watch the performance. She matched Bebe's every move with a slight movement of her own accompanied by a silent prayer.

Bebe turned her door handle. No problem. She pushed against the door. It didn't budge. She pushed harder. The door didn't open, but the entire car started to sway.

"Whoa, Baby," Fonnie whispered.

"You talking to me or the car or the Good Lord?"

"Anybody that's listening." Fonnie exhaled like a collapsing balloon. "On second thought, suppose you help me crawl over to your side first. That will give us more ballast to tip the car toward the road and away from the abyss."

"You think?"

"You pull my left arm and I'll push with my right. If I can get my petite bottom over the emergency brake in the middle, I can shove against you while you shove the door." It wasn't easy, but little by little Fonnie inched her hips to the left, straddled the metal bar, carefully lifted her left leg over the gear shift. During the maneuvers the car dipped and swayed like a small boat in a big storm. Fonnie felt the beginnings of seasickness.

Bebe clutched tighter to her friend's left hand. "You all right?"

Fonnie grunted. Fear seized her throat making speech impossible.

Bebe took a deep breath. "I'll count to three. Then I'll slam myself against the door and you push against me with all your might."

Fonnie steeled herself.

Bebe started counting. "One. Two." She stopped and looked wildly around. "Wait. My purse. Where's my purse?"

"Who cares about your damned purse?" Fonnie's tattered nerves were beyond humor or civility. She felt like she was going to disgrace herself soon by bursting into tears.

"My cell phone. It's in my purse. We'll need it to call for help after we get out."

Fonnie thought about that for a second, shifted her eyes to the floor. "I think it's behind your right foot. But there's no way I'm going to reach down there and get it."

"Then I will. I need my phone."

Before Fonnie could react, Bebe dropped her hand, dove over and down, swooped up her purse, and came up with a triumphant smile. The smile didn't last long. The Camry groaned, shimmied, flirted with the rocks below. Bebe lunged against her door. Fonnie reeled to the left.

The door ripped open, Bebe's torso toppled out, her right hand still gripping her purse. She clung to the door handle as she eased her legs out and under her. Then in one fluid motion, she abandoned the purse, reached up, grabbed Fonnie's arm and hauled her across the seat. Fonnie propped her good right foot against the gear shift and gave a mighty shove. It propelled her nearly out of the car. Bebe finished the job with a final tug and both of them landed on the roadway.

The Camry gave one massive tremor and tipped up at a forty-five degree angle. But to Fonnie's surprise it didn't plunge over into the crevasse. "That guardrail must have been stouter than I thought." When Bebe made no comment, Fonnie looked at her companion. Bebe was sprawled back like a filleted catfish, her eyes shut, her breathing shallow. Fonnie flipped over on her knees, crawled close to Bebe's head, slapped her on the cheek. "Wake up already. We're out! We're safe. At least we will be as soon as we get out of the road."

Bebe opened her eyes and said in a soft voice. "If you don't mind, I was in the middle of a silent thanks-giving prayer."

Fonnie sat back on her heels. "Sorry to interrupt your communion with the Almighty. But it's cold and it'll be dark in about an hour, so I suggest we find that cell phone of yours, hope to goodness it works, and get some human help out here."

Bebe jerked up. "Good idea."

They both scrambled to their feet. Bebe retrieved her purse and dug around its contents for her cell phone. They made their way to the opposite side of the road from where the Camry dangled precariously. Bebe found the phone, flipped it open, and let out a loud groan.

Fonnie looked worried. "What's the matter? Is it broken?"

Bebe shook her head. "No. Out of range."

Fonnie's exhilaration of getting out of the car in one piece began to evaporate. "You mean we can't call from here?"

"Not from where I'm standing." Bebe looked around. "We're in a hollow. Maybe if I climb up to higher ground, I could get through." She studied the terrain some more, then pointed to a rocky bluff above their heads. "I'll try that area."

"And leave me here alone? What if Mr. Black Honda Man comes back to finish his botched job?"

"He's not coming back. Besides, I think he just intended to scare us, not kill us." Bebe climbed over the guardrail and started trudging up the slope. She called back, "Don't worry, I'll have you in my sight at all times."

"A fat lot of good that'll do, with you halfway up the mountain." Fonnie found a large smooth rock to sit on and tried to think good thoughts. It wasn't easy. The pleasant breeze they'd enjoyed all day was now becoming brisk and cold, the afternoon shadows were lengthening, and her right ankle was beginning to ache. She must have wrenched it getting out of the car.

But before she could embark on a full-fledged pity-party, Bebe's cheery voice floated down. "I got it. I called 911. They're sending out a tow truck. I told them we didn't need an ambulance."

Fonnie hollered back to her. "Call my home phone and leave a message for Brian. Tell him I'll be a little late, but not to worry."

"That's all you're going to tell him?"

"That's all he needs to know for now."

A STATE POLICE VEHICLE arrived in a short while followed by a tow truck. Bebe told the two officers that for some unknown reason a man in a black Honda—she thought it was an Accord— ran them off the road. "It had a North Carolina tag. I noticed that when he roared past, but only caught the first letter. I think it was an M or an N."

"Can you describe the driver?" the older officer asked.

"Not really," Bebe said. "Big. Wore a baseball cap. Couldn't see his face much."

"But you're sure it was a man?"

"Well, yes—I guess so." Bebe turned to Fonnie. "You got a better look than I did. What do you think?"

Fonnie was still sitting on her boulder pedestal. The policemen came closer as she answered. "The driver was big. I'm sure it was a man. I didn't get a good look at his face, but he looked dark. You know, had a dark complexion. I couldn't see any hair. I guess the cap covered it all. But he seemed mad."

"What do you mean 'mad'?"

"Angry," Fonnie said. "He was hunched over the wheel like he was furious with us."

The younger officer turned back to Bebe, "Do you think he ran you off the road deliberately?"

Bebe shrugged. "I thought so at the time, but I could have been wrong. Maybe he was just in a hurry, and I was holding him up. Maybe he had a fight with his wife and was taking it out on us. Could have been a simple case of road rage."

"Maybe," the older officer said. "Did you do anything to aggravate him?"

"Not that I know of. My friend and I were just taking our time, talking, enjoying the scenery."

"Not much scenery this time of year," the younger officer remarked. He studied the driver's license that Bebe had handed him. "You're quite a distance from home. What brought you up this way today."

"Just visiting some old friends."

Fonnie held her breath, hoped he didn't ask for names. He didn't. "I need to see your car's registration too," he said.

"It's probably in the glove compartment."

"Probably? Don't you know?"

"Well, you see, it's not my car. I just borrowed it for the day from a friend."

The officer glanced at the lopsided car balancing on the guard rail and at the tow truck driver who was attempting to hook onto the back bumper. "A good friend, I hope."

"Me too."

The older officer approached Fonnie again. "You have any ID on you? We'll have to file a report."

"It's in my handbag in the car. My cane's in there too. I hope that fella knows what he's doing or the whole thing could end up in the gully."

The officer smiled. "You needn't worry about Ernie. He's an expert at getting cars back on the road. Actually, it doesn't look like a lot of damage. A couple of dents, out of alignment, but probably driveable."

It didn't take Ernie long to pull the Camry off the guardrail and set all four of its tires on the black top. He crawled under the car and played a flashlight around. "No major damage here," he called out. He scrambled out, jumped behind the wheel, and started the motor. He drove a short distance, then turned around. "It oughta get you home. Just don't go too fast, or it may get to wobbling. Of course, if you want me to, I can tow it to my garage and give it a better look-see."

"No, if you think it's safe to drive, I'll take your word for it." Bebe pulled out her checkbook. "How much do I owe you?"

She then turned to the officers. "So can we go now?"

"As soon as you show me the car's registration."

Bebe reached in the glove compartment, offered him the card and then brought out Fonnie's cane. Fonnie grasped the cane and made her way to the passenger side door.

"Just a minute, Ma'am," the older officer said, "I still need to see your ID. Just to be sure I get everything right on the report."

Fonnie scrambled into her seat, snatched up her purse, and handed the officer her driver's license.

He studied the license, looked at Fonnie, and then back to the piece of plastic. "This is expired."

"I know. I don't drive anymore. I just keep it for old time's sake. It's still good for ID, isn't it?"

The officer grinned. "Not really. You've changed your hair-do."

"True, but my wrinkles are the same. A person can't fake those."

Smiling, he handed the license back. "So long, ladies. Have a good trip home."

IT WAS A QUIET TRIP until they were well into North Carolina. Fonnie broke the silence. "I guess we'll have to tell the whole story to Mike and Brian."

"I think that's the best plan. Do you want me to come in with you when you talk with Brian?"

"No. I can still handle that boy. He'll just threaten to have me committed or to send me back to Springwillow."

"Or make you promise not to associate with me anymore."

"That too."

Bebe tapped her fingers on the steering wheel. "I think we can wait until tomorrow to call Lieutenant Dickson. You can let me know when he wants to meet with us. But we're not going to cower and apologize. In fact he should thank us for helping in the investigation."

"That'll be the day."

Fonnie was quiet as questions swirled around in her

head. She turned in her seat so she could study Bebe's profile. "Level with me. What do you really think happened this afternoon? And don't try that road rage bit on me. Maybe those Virginia state troopers bought it, but I can't."

"Me either. I really think we were being warned off. We're supposed to leave Christine in her grave and not try to figure out who put her there."

"And are we going to do that?"

Bebe gave Fonnie a full-face smile. "Well, like the little pig told the big bad wolf, 'Not by the hair of your chinny-chin-chin.'"

SEVENTEEN

WHEN BEBE DROVE UP to her house she was surprised to see Neil Vincent's SUV parked on the street and Neil sitting on the front stoop clutching a bouquet of Gerber daisies. She parked in her drive and started up the walk. Neil hurried to meet her. "Thank God you're all right!" He grabbed her in a quick hug, then just as quickly released her and stood back to look at her more closely. "You are all right, aren't you? I was so worried."

Bebe's emotions zigzagged from annoyance to pleasure to suspicion. "Why shouldn't I be all right? And what are you doing here?"

Neil dropped his eyes to the flowers in his hand. "I came to bring you these." He shoved the colorful flowers toward her. When she didn't reach out for them, he dropped his outstretched hand. The yellow and orange daisies brushed against his brown trousers. "Actually, I came to apologize."

"Apologize for what?" Bebe watched in amusement as Neil squirmed. Good. *He deserves to squirm,* she thought. She hadn't wanted to admit it, even to herself, but his absence from the memorial service had hurt her deeply. She was more than ready to accept his apology for it, but at the same time, she worried about him being worried about her. What did he know about her trip today, about her road encounter? She waited in silence for him to answer her question.

"How about inviting me in? I'll explain everything." When she didn't respond, he brought the now bedraggled bouquet up again. "These poor devils need some water, and I could use some coffee. What about it?"

Bebe finally relented, gave him a polite smile, motioned toward the front door. Once inside she found a vase for the flowers and put the kettle on to heat. "It'll have to be instant. I'm out of the other and I didn't have time to shop this weekend." She studied him as she reached for the coffee mugs. "But of course, you know all about my weekend, all about my travels. So go ahead. Explain."

"First of all, I didn't participate in your little detective foray because I thought it not only foolish, but dangerous. The same thing goes for the service you concocted. You were putting yourself out there as a friend of a murdered person. Christine Hauner was killed for a purpose. Didn't you realize that the murderer might be looking for another victim?"

"No. My only thought was to honor a person who had very little going for her in this life and whose death needed to be acknowledged. I wasn't concerned about my own safety, but I can certainly understand your concern. You didn't want to be associated with a bunch of nuts."

"That's not fair. I'm just not a foolhardy person."

"And I am?"

Neil took two quick gulps of coffee. "Let's just say you don't always think through your actions."

"Like my trip today. Would you like to explain how you know about that?"

"I will if you knock that chip off your shoulder and give me half a chance."

"Okay. I guess I deserve that. I'm listening. My mind is open."

"Good. First, between classes this morning I called the bookstore to apologize for the weekend. Frankly, I thought you would be a bit more understanding than you appear to be. But anyway, when I got the recording about the store being closed, I thought you were probably just resting up at home. So I called here and got another recording." Neil glanced over to the answering machine where the red light was doing a polka. "I left you a nice message you can listen to later."

Bebe peeked over to the blinking light and rewarded Neil with a quick grin. "Go on."

"I called again on my lunch break. Still no answer. Didn't leave a message that time. I figured you'd gone shopping or something. When you still didn't answer when school was out, I drove over. I suddenly sensed something was wrong." Neil stared into his nearly empty cup. He seemed to falter over his next words. "Do you believe that certain people have a connection? That somehow their minds and emotions can mesh across a distance?" Neil stared into Bebe's startled eyes. "I think that's what happened to me. I sensed you were in danger, that you were scared."

Bebe's mind was making like a whirlygig and she whispered. "What time was that?"

"About four." He downed the rest of his coffee. "Bebe, what was happening to you at four o'clock?"

She shook her head. Her fists clenched as they had been clenched on the steering wheel, her heart pounded as her mind again relived the moment the black car rammed her car, her body swayed just as the Camry had swayed when it straddled the broken guardrail. She took a deep breath. "I'll tell you later. It's your story now. What did you do then?"

Neil slid back in his chair, brushed some flower fragments from his jacket. "I tried to ignore the feeling. Thought I was being melodramatic. I decided to go to the flower shop, buy you a little peace offering and figured when I got back, you'd be here. You know what I saw when I got to Betty's Greenhouse?"

Bebe nodded. "My truck."

"That's right. I hurried in, expecting you to be there. When you weren't, I asked Betty where you were. She explained about you borrowing her car to go to Virginia. She said you had just called, that you'd had an accident and would be late getting home. She said she told you not to bother to return the car tonight, so I came here to wait for you. I was so worried."

"Didn't Betty tell you I wasn't hurt."

"Yes, but I wasn't sure you'd tell her the truth. Anyway, I got the flowers and I've been sitting here ever since—imagining all sorts of things. I knew Christine was originally from Virginia so it was obvious your trip had to do with her. And to me, that meant you were putting yourself in danger again."

Neil hunched forward. Bebe had the distinct impression that he wanted to hold her hand, and she wasn't sure she was ready for that. She scooted back further on the couch. She appreciated Neil's concern for her, hoped it was genuine, but doubts about him jumped around in her brain. Had he really sensed she was in danger? She did believe that certain people had spiritual connections that could transcend space and time, but she never imagined that she and Neil could fall into that category. They were too different. Or were they? She had to admit she was attracted to him physically, but his refusal to officially join CATWAG had disappointed her. Maybe she'd misjudged him. Perhaps he was just an independent thinker, and she could admire him for that. She'd have to ponder on it, but not now—she was too tired.

Neil's voice interrupted her thoughts. "Your turn now. What did happen today? And what did you learn in Virginia?"

Bebe gave him an abbreviated version of the day's events. She downplayed the road incident and suggested the road rage explanation was probably correct. If he was really worried about her, she didn't want to add to his alarm by bringing up the possibility of it being a warning. When he seemed to be calmed down, she leaned back and patted her mouth in a yawn. "It's been a long day. I didn't realize I was so tired. I really do thank you for your concern—and the flowers. But right now I think I need a hot shower and my bed."

Neil nodded as he stood up. "Sure. I'll call you tomorrow."

"That'll be nice."

BRIAN WAS GETTING READY to go out when Fonnie came in. "Have a good day?" he called as he scuttled down the stairs. Without waiting for an answer, he added, "I'm meeting some buddies for pizza and study. Got a big test tomorrow. Hope you ate dinner before coming home."

Fonnie headed for the den, flopped down on the sofa. "Oh, sure, I've eaten." It wasn't exactly a lie, she reasoned. They had eaten, even though it had been hours earlier. Right now she was too tired to be hungry anyway. "You run along. I'll probably be in bed by the time you get home."

For a while Fonnie thought she was going to get out of explaining her day to Brian. But she knew the "jig was up" when he peeked his head in the doorway, gave a jerk, came over to stand in front of her and stared at the grimy, torn knees of her slacks. "Good Lord, what happened to you?"

Fonnie looked down at her ruined pants. How could she explain crawling around on her hands and knees? "Would you believe an old fashioned extended prayer meeting?"

Brian shook his head. "With you I'd believe almost anything, but I'd like the truth."

So Fonnie told him the truth, every last bit of it. He listened quietly, rolled his eyes a couple of times, made occasional moaning sounds. When she got to the part of the car chase, he started pacing the floor, and when she recounted about dangling over the guard rail, he threw up his hands and groaned. He calmed down a bit when she mentioned the state policemen. "So you did file a police report about the attempt on your lives."

"Not exactly."

"What do you mean—not exactly?"

"Bebe and I didn't think it was an attempt on our lives. We figured it was just an attempt to scare us off from the investigation. Actually, we told the police it was probably road rage and that no harm was done." Fonnie gave Brian a grandmotherly smile meant to convey that she had everything under control. "Now you run along and study hard. I'll call Lieutenant Dickson in the morning and explain everything to him. He can do whatever follow up needs to be done."

"And you and Bebe will stay out of it?"

"Of course."

Brian headed for the door, stopped, and turned

around. He sat down next to his grandmother and took her hands in his. "You've got to listen to me, Gram. This isn't a game. You may have put yourself in real danger. Promise me you won't do anything else foolish."

Fonnie was taken aback by Brian's seriousness. She hated to see him worried like that. "I promise I won't leave the house without telling you where I'm going, with whom and why. Okay?"

"Okay. Oh, and you have a message on the answering machine from Ed Whitehall. He wants to come over to see you."

"That's nice. I'd like to talk to him." Fonnie gave Brian a demure smile. "That is, if you approve."

Brian laughed. "I guess it's all right—if he comes while Keisha's here."

After Brian left, Fonnie pushed the answering machine button. She wanted to hear for herself what Ed had to say.

"Mrs. Beachum, this is Ed Whitehall. I was hoping I could come over sometime tomorrow and talk with you. I happen to have a rare day when I'm in town and nothing pressing going on in the office. Please give me a call if this meets your approval." Fonnie jotted down the telephone number, but headed for the kitchen and a cup of tea before calling him back.

While waiting for the microwave to ping, she replayed Whitehall's message in her head. She couldn't imagine what he wanted from her, but she wasn't going to pass up an opportunity to grill him. She decided to ask him over in the morning and to defer talking to Mike until the afternoon.

Fonnie placed her tea and two oatmeal cookies on her tea cart, shoved the cart over to the desk and made the call. Ed quickly agreed to an eleven o'clock meeting. That would give her plenty of time to get ready and for Keisha to do her work.

Since she was already at the computer desk and the screen was beckoning to her, Fonnie felt it was time to update her journal. Putting words in front of her face always clarified her thoughts. She still had to type with one hand, but she had learned to position her left hand on the keyboard and she could occasionally type letters with her left middle finger. It was slow and frustrating work and she usually ended up placing the flaccid hand back in her lap to give her right hand free rein.

October 27

A long exhausting day. Bebe and I visited Christine's grave in VA. We found out 1) her daughter died with a malignant brain tumor (Mike already told us that) 2) Christine blamed the cancer on drinking water poisoned by landfill leakage. Landfill run by Myerson. She confronted some of Myerson officials. 3) her ex-husband and oldest son work at landfill. This caused split in the family. Important info, but probably nothing that points to the murderer. So why were we followed and run off the road? Do we really know more than we realize? Driver wasn't anyone we recognized. Couldn't catch the license plate number. Maybe we imagined whole thing. A black sedan is a black sedan—they're everywhere. Maybe it really was a case of road rage as we told the police officers.

Enough! I've got to think about Ed Whitehall.

*A successful business man, well thought of in com-
munity. But there's something peculiar about him.
I know he lied about what a nice person Christine
was. A person doesn't have a morning personality
and a different one for afternoons. He obviously
thinks Christine told me something that could in-
criminate Myerson and endanger the landfill
contract. Perhaps I ought to play into that idea. I
could pretend to know something and lead him on.
He may let something slip—like why he supports
Myerson so much. Maybe he's getting a payoff
from them. Maybe—*

Fonnie's head began to nod. Her brain had shut
down. It was time to lock up and call it a night. She
clicked the print button but didn't wait to retrieve the
paper. She put the chain on the front door, wobbled into
her bedroom, struggled into her nightgown.

She slept fitfully, her night filled with dreams of
black cars, bottled water, and golden chrysanthemums
on a child's grave.

EIGHTEEN

IN SPITE OF a restless night Fonnie awoke with her brain in full gear and her determination intact. She wanted to get this investigation over with and get her life back on an even keel. Brian had already left when she shambled into the kitchen. Her walking had been improving lately but yesterday's adventure left her with sore muscles and a more decided limp. She was sure she'd feel better after she had coffee and breakfast.

Brian had made a pot of coffee and poured some into a pint thermos for her. Bless him, she thought. He knew she loved perked coffee in the morning but that she had a hard time pouring it from the big pot. She doctored it up with real sugar and took a sip as she turned on the morning news.

"Mild today, rain starting tonight, colder tomorrow. The forecast for Halloween weekend looks good for ghosts and goblins—mild and clear." Halloween already? My how time flies when you're having fun. Fonnie hoped Brian planned to be home Halloween night to open the door to trick-or-treaters. She doubted she would want to do it on her own.

Her attention came back to the TV reporter when she heard the word, "burglaries." "Two more break-ins have been reported, both on the west side of town. As in all the previous ones, the houses were either unoccupied or the owners out of town. No fingerprints or clues found, and the burglars took only things that could be carried easily such as silverware and jewelry. A police spokesman stated that none of the property from previous robberies has been recovered, and it's assumed the stolen goods were disposed of in distant cities."

Fonnie had been too busy lately to think of her own missing silverware and poor kidnapped Leopold. Now tears shimmered in her eyes. "I bet they're not even trying to find you, Leopold. Why should the police be concerned with my little unicorn?" She took another swallow of coffee and swiped her eyes. "I hope you're bringing some comfort into someone else's life—if you haven't already been melted down."

The reporter went on to world events without any mention of the murder investigation or the landfill controversy. Fonnie turned off the TV as Keisha knocked on the kitchen door, then let herself in. Fonnie had given her a key just in case. She didn't elaborate on what 'just in case' meant, but Keisha understood.

Keisha took one look at Fonnie and shook her head. "You look like you've been out on an all-night binge. Hair tangled, eyes red, skin blotchy."

"And good morning to you, too, Little Miss Sunshine."

"I'm sorry. There's nothing wrong with you that a good long bath, a shampoo, and a little makeup can't cure. Then you can fill me in on your trip yesterday. Tyrone already told me all about the weekend activities. I guess that wasn't enough excitement for you, was it?"

"Aren't you the one that told me I needed to do more for myself? So I've formed a committee of one to get me out of the house more often. Does that suit you?"

Keisha laughed as she came up behind Fonnie and

gave her a bear hug. "It certainly does. Now let me fix you some breakfast, then I'll run your bath water."

By ten o'clock Fonnie was scrubbed, combed, made up, and dressed in a lemon yellow sweat suit. "Now you look like you're ready to take on the world again."

"But is the world ready for me?"

Fonnie's next task was to call the police station. She asked for Detective Dickson. "May I say who's calling?"

"Fonnie Beachum. Tell him I have more information about the Hauner case."

The wait seemed interminable but finally a deep voice came on the line. It wasn't Mike. "Mrs. Beachum. Lieutenant Dickson isn't available right now. This is Officer Zimmer. Can I help you?"

Fonnie was taken aback. She wanted Mike to know what had happened yesterday, but she wasn't sure it should go through a third party. "Please tell him that someone tried to kill Bebe Englehook and me yesterday." She knew it was probably a lie when she told it, but she had no doubt it would get Mike's attention and a prompt response.

She heard Officer Zimmer's quick intake of breath before he stammered. "Perhaps you'd better tell me the details."

"Can't right now. I'm expecting company soon. Tell Mike to call me back after lunch." Before the officer could say anything else, she hung up. That'll teach the big detective not to take my calls, she thought. I bet anything he was standing right there all the time.

Fonnie half expected the phone to ring right back with Mike demanding to know what she was talking about. When that didn't happen, she found a dust cloth and busied herself grooming the remaining unicorns in her collection. As she did, she tried to remember the history behind each one: birthdays, anniversaries, gifts not only from Harrison, but from her brother, from Amy, and from various friends who knew of her quirky collection. They were all precious and she felt a little guilty about grieving so much for Leopold and not enjoying the ones that were left. As she dusted, she rearranged them to fill up the vacant space left by Leopold. It was her way of saying goodbye to her loyal friend.

A knock on the front door surprised her. She glanced at the wall clock. Five to eleven. Either Ed Whitehall was early or her clock was slow. It didn't matter. As she hurried to the front door, she passed the computer and noticed her journal entry of the night before. She snatched the paper from the printer and quickly skimmed the contents before sliding it into a desk drawer. It wouldn't do for Ed to see what she'd written. She pondered her idea about leading Ed to believe that Christine had told her some big dark secret. But would that fall into the "foolish" category Brian had warned her about? Perhaps so. She'd have to see how things played out. At any rate, she'd only promised Brian to let him know when she went out. Surely nothing bad could happen in her own home.

Another knock sounded. Keisha poked her head out of the hall bathroom. "Do you want me to get that?"

"No. Just keep on with your cleaning. It would be nice, though, if you could make us some fresh coffee in a little."

Fonnie unhooked the chain, opened the door, invited her guest in. Ed was dressed in a gray business suit with a pale blue shirt and a blue-striped tie. He tipped his head, gave her a wide smile, "Good morning. Lovely day, isn't it?"

"Yes. Lovely." Fonnie inhaled the warm, fresh air and whatever after-shave lotion Ed was wearing with equal pleasure. "Come on in the den. So nice of you to call on me."

She led the way to the sofa, sat on the far end, and motioned for him to have a seat in the recliner. Instead of sitting down, Ed wandered around the room, as if studying her decor. It was labeled Early American, but probably should have been more honestly titled early thrift shop.

His eyes came to rest on the shelves of unicorns. "Interesting. You're a collector?"

"Not really. They're just gifts from various people. Apparently I'm hard to buy for and the idea of giving me unicorns kind of spread throughout the family." Fonnie shrugged her shoulders. "Rather silly, actually."

Ed didn't argue the point but moved toward the dining room. "I love old houses. I dabble in real estate, you know. Mostly rentals."

"Oh? I thought you ran a travel agency."

"I do. Mainly I set up speciality tours. People with special interests love to go on vacations featuring their passions." Ed continued his surveillance of the room, peeked into the kitchen. "For instance, I have a tour for book lovers featuring homes of famous authors. And there's a tour featuring houses with live-in ghosts and apparitions. Of course, the Nashville Music tour is always popular."

"Is that why you travel so much—setting up the tours?"

"Yes. I enjoy it and I can write it off as a business expense. Speaking of traveling, you must have taken a little trip yourself yesterday. I called several times and you weren't home."

"You called several times? But there was only one message."

"That was when I had given up hope of reaching you and decided to make it another day. Did you have a nice outing?"

"Yes. Went to visit an old friend." Fonnie wasn't about to confide in someone she wasn't sure she could trust.

"Good. I'm glad you were able to get out. There's no friend like an old friend."

Fonnie decided the polite chit-chat had gone on long enough. She wasn't learning anything new about the Myerson Corporation, and she knew Ed had not gotten around to the real purpose of his visit. "So, you're not busy and you decided to pay me a visit. Why?"

Her abruptness seemed to catch him off-guard. He stopped his pacing, came over and sat down on the other end of the sofa. He gave her the kind of smile she assumed he'd perfected to sell one of his tours to a cautious buyer. "As I said at the memorial service, Christine had spoken so highly of you I wanted to get better acquainted."

"Cut the crap, Ed. Christine never spoke highly of anybody—including you. What do you really want?"

Ed pushed up with his hands, then slid further back into the corner of the sofa. "All right. What I really want to know is what Christine did say about me. She didn't seem to like me. I have no idea why, but she didn't. As you can imagine, my business depends on people liking me and trusting me and I can't take the chance of any bad karma."

"And you didn't think your association with Myerson and your backing of the new landfill would result in bad karma?"

"Why should it? Dale Myerson is a fine upstanding businessman, and his company has been unfairly maligned. Ms. Franklin assured me there was nothing valid about the safety complaints alleged by CATWAG."

"And you believed her? Or did she buy your county commissioner vote with a hefty payoff?"

"Nonsense."

"Is that what Christine suspected?" Fonnie went on. "And you're afraid she might have mentioned it to me?"

Keisha picked that particular moment to carry in a tray with coffee and cookies, thus halting the conversation. She placed the tray on the coffee table. "Good morning, Mr. Whitehall. I'm Keisha Riggs. It's so nice to meet you. I do admire people who take their civic duty seriously." She set a coffee mug in front of him along with the sugar and creamer. He nodded acknowledgment, but didn't make any comment. Keisha went on. "Serving on the county board must be so time consuming, what with all your business interests."

Again Ed Whitehall nodded. He cleared his throat. "Yes, indeed. It is time consuming, but I feel I owe it to the community."

"And we appreciate it." She shoved the plate of cookies closer. "Do try the macaroons. They're delightful."

Fonnie stared at Keisha in puzzlement. There was something behind all these pleasantries. What was she up to?

Keisha turned as if she was leaving, then did an about-face. "By the way, I couldn't help but overhear Fonnie's question to you." She paused while Mr. Whitehall bit into the crunchy coconut goodie. "*Did* you take a bribe from Ms. Franklin?"

Fonnie covered her mouth to suppress a giggle while

Ed gave a short choking sound. He recovered quickly, took a sip of coffee and seemed to force the corners of his mouth up into something that resembled a smile. "No, young lady. I did not take a payoff or bribe or anything of the sort. And I assure you that Lanie Franklin and Dale Myerson are too respectable to be involved in anything underhanded."

"Good. I'm glad to hear it. Well, time for me to be off." She looked at Fonnie. "All right if I go?"

"Of course, dear. See you in the morning."

Ed waited until he heard the back door slam, took another sip of coffee, then rose. "I should be going also. I'm sorry our visit couldn't have been more pleasant."

Instantly Fonnie felt guilty. Ed Whitehall was a perfectly fine gentleman and she hadn't been very nice to him. "I'm sorry too, Ed. Sometimes my imagination runs away with me. I had no right to suggest you've done anything wrong. And to ease your mind, I assure you Christine never said anything against you. In fact, she said very little all the time she worked here. She wasn't a person who communicated freely."

Ed rubbed the back of his neck, his eyes again roaming the room. "Thank you. I guess I was worried over nothing." He headed toward the hallway. "Thanks for the coffee. Nice place you have here. If you ever want to rent or sell, just let me know."

Fonnie got up and followed Ed to the door. She gave him a sheepish smile. "I'm afraid I wasn't a very good hostess. And I didn't even ask about your mother. How is she doing? I assume you have another aide for her."

"Yes. She's a little young—but competent. Mother seems comfortable with her."

"That's good. I'd like to meet your mother. Perhaps I could come over to your house one day."

"Well, you understand that Mother's mind is confused." Ed hesitated. "She doesn't really know what's going on and she isn't up to having company."

Fonnie smiled. "Sometimes old people can surprise you. They often know more than they are given credit for."

Ed opened the door and was halfway out when he responded. "I suppose you're right. Maybe it would be nice if you visited. I could come over and get you one day. I'll give you a call."

"I'll look forward to it."

NINETEEN

THE DOOR OF the Second Chance Book Store opened
and shut. Bebe looked up from reviewing last week's
receipts to greet a customer. "Detective Dickson. Good
morning. Looking for a good mystery book?"

The detective shook his head, leaned over the
counter, picked up a book titled *Myths and Magic*, set
it back down. "Just looking for some answers."

"To what questions?"

"To why Mrs. Beachum claimed someone tried to
kill the two of you yesterday. And what you were up to
when it happened. And why you didn't let me know immediately." He picked up a paperweight filled with
water and three swimming dolphins, turned it upside
down, watched the dolphins right themselves.

"Cute, eh?" Bebe said. "No matter which way you
turn it, the dolphins always have their heads up looking
right at you." She knew the detective wasn't interested in
the dolphins, but she was playing for time to come up with
her answers. "I understand they're pretty smart animals."

"That's right. They learn from experience. Something some humans fail to do."

Bebe stepped back a little, took off her reading
glasses. "What's that supposed to mean?"

"I thought you understood the police were handling
the Hauner investigation."

"Of course. I understand that."

"So why the trip to Virginia?"

Bebe took another step back, found the stool she kept behind the counter, and plopped down. "How did you know about that?" She sat straight up as a weird thought vaulted into her head. "You had us followed? It was your man in the black car?"

Dickson raised his eyebrows. "No. I didn't have you followed. Although that might not be such a bad idea from now on."

"Then how?"

"The Virginia state police sent our state police a copy of an accident report because the cars were from North Carolina. We were given the report since the incident involved citizens of our county. The report, however, said you were victims of road rage. But I assumed there was more to it than that."

"Then you haven't talked to Fonnie yet?"

"No. She called and left a message about attempted murder. I thought I'd get your take on it first. Now tell me all about the trip and exactly what happened."

"You look tired." Bebe motioned to another stool behind the counter. "Come around and take a load off. This is going to be a long story."

The lieutenant accepted the offered stool, took out his notebook and scribbled notes as the tale unfolded. He interrupted a few times with questions, "You didn't see the car yourself in the cemetery?" and "You can't describe the man driving at all?" and "You're sure it was the same car that was in front of your house?" Each time Bebe shook her head for a negative answer.

When she finished her story, he asked, "Where's your car now—that is, the one you were driving?"

"In Simpson's body shop. I told Betty I'd pay for the repairs and a new paint job myself. It wouldn't be right to put a claim against her insurance."

"Call and tell them not to do anything to the car until I get a look at it."

Bebe reached for the phone. "Sure, but I don't know how that will help you."

"Can't tell. There might be paint specks from the black car. At any rate, I like to cover all the bases."

When she hung up the phone, Bebe turned back to Dickson. "So what do you think?"

He picked up the dolphin paperweight again and watched them swirl in the water. "I think you had better take a lesson from the dolphins. They have enough sense to stay away from danger."

After the detective left, Bebe realized he'd made no comment about the information they had learned from Sybil. Didn't he think it significant that the Myerson landfill in Emmetsville was suspected of contaminating the ground water and that Christine blamed the company for her daughter's death?

AFTER ED LEFT, his mention of Lanie Franklin stayed in Fonnie's mind. He'd described her as a very respectable person. Actually that had been Fonnie's impression when she'd first seen the Myerson vice-president on TV. She was as tall as a man, a little overweight, African-American. Any or all of these factors could have made her socially insecure, but she had exuded poise and self-confidence, and yes, an image of re-spectability. This image was marred the day she and Dale Myerson had joined Fonnie for lunch.

Ms. Franklin had become defensive when Fonnie

mentioned the corporation's safety violations alleged by CATWAG. At the time, Fonnie didn't know if there was any substance to the allegations. Now, thanks to Sybil's information, she did. Sybil had said that although Myerson did not admit any guilt about the Emmetsville landfill having a leakage problem, they did pay a fine and installed a new lining in the site. She wondered how Lanie would explain that. Maybe I should call her, Fonnie thought, and see how she responds.

Before she had a chance to dissuade herself from this action, Fonnie snatched up the telephone directory, found the motel number, and quickly dialed. She asked for Lanie Franklin's room, knowing that she may not be in, but if not, Fonnie would leave a message asking her to call.

The desk clerk squashed that plan. "I'm sorry. Ms. Franklin checked out early yesterday morning." Then he added before she asked, "And all of the other Myerson personnel checked out in the afternoon."

"All right. Thank you." On further thought, Fonnie decided their departures were a logical step for the company. All construction on the landfill was probably suspended until the police finished their investigation. Or perhaps, as Bebe had hoped, the Environmental League had successfully filed an injunction against further progress. At any rate, Lanie and her underlings had probably gone back to their corporate headquarters, as Dale had done earlier.

Fonnie scrambled around in the desk drawer looking for the business card Dale had given her the day of his visit. It was probably in the pile of bills and papers that had been scattered during Sunday's break-in. She'd shoved everything in the desk, planning on doing a neater job later on. She found the card and the corporate office number. Might as well give it a try.

"I'm sorry Ms. Franklin isn't in," the Myerson operator said. "She's taking a few days off. If you care to leave a message I'll give you her voice mail."

"Never mind," Fonnie said. Her thoughts were swirling around in her head. She wanted to find out if Lanie had gone into the office the day before. "I called yesterday and left a message on her voice mail. Do you know if she got it?" Fonnie was pleased at how easily the lie flew past her lips. Man, I'm good, she thought.

"I don't know. She didn't come in, but she may have called in and retrieved her messages."

"Thank you. If I don't hear from her, I'll call later in the week."

Feeling some hunger pangs, she made her way to the kitchen. Keisha had started leaving her a sandwich or salad in the refrigerator. Fonnie had dismissed the Meals on Wheels she had when she first came home. She appreciated the volunteers who brought the lunches, but preferred her own food.

As she munched on the roast beef sandwich, she envisioned Lanie at some cozy beach house, feet propped up, staring at the blowing sand dunes, trying to erase Groverton from her mind.

Fonnie figured she might as well have another macaroon. The bits of coconut sometimes got caught between her teeth, but the delicious crunch was worth an extra brushing. Hoping to catch the weather report, she turned on the TV. The wind was picking up and she wouldn't be surprised to hear of an expected temperature drop.

Instead of Winnie the Weather Girl, the somber face of the anchor man filled the screen. "This report just in. Lanie Franklin, vice-president of the Myerson Corporation, has been found dead from a gun shot wound, apparently self-inflicted. Her body was found in her car at the entrance to the proposed landfill site. There was no evidence of a struggle." The newsman looked down, shuffled some papers, stared back into the camera. "We'll bring you further information as we learn it. Now back to the weather."

Fonnie sat stunned. Her mind seemed incapable of taking in the information her ears had just heard. Lanie Franklin dead? Self-inflicted? Impossible. But that's what the grim newscaster had said. And at the landfill site. How did that tie in with Christine's death?

Fonnie reached for the remote. She no longer cared about the weather. At the moment she felt that the sun might never again shine in Groverton.

She grabbed two aspirins off the counter where Brian kept a supply. He often complained of a headache when he came home. She knew he was working and studying too hard and she worried about him. But right now she was glad the painkillers were handy as she gulped them down. She grasped her cane and headed for the den sofa. She needed to lie down and put her brain in neutral for at least a short while.

It didn't happen. Her body was resting, but her brain refused to stop spinning. She stopped expecting a call from Mike about the message she'd left for him this morning. He was far too busy now with another body. But wait, if Lanie's death was a suicide, there would be no reason for the homicide detective to be involved. Even as this thought skittered around in her head, she knew it wasn't valid. Because Lanie's death, even if a suicide, had to be connected to the murder.

Fonnie threw back the afghan and sat up. In fact, maybe this was the solution to the murder. Lanie killed Christine and then killed herself out of remorse, or out of fear of detection. Fonnie had to get up. She hurried over to the computer. She had to get her thoughts on paper. Maybe they would make more sense then. She didn't bother with a date or introduction to her subject or any grammar niceties.

Lanie could have killed Christine. She was big and strong enough to overpower the smaller woman. She could have moved her into a car and dumped her body at the landfill. Taking her to the landfill would cast suspicion on someone who opposed it. Then Lanie's conscience bothered her so much she couldn't bear it, and she killed herself.

Makes sense, but too pat? Did Lanie leave a note admitting Christine's murder or a suicide note of any kind. She was an executive—organized, precise. She wouldn't have killed herself without being sure the reason was clear. Or did she do it in a fit of depression—wasn't thinking clearly?

Or yet, maybe it wasn't suicide. The TV man said 'apparent' whatever that means.

Fonnie's headache was getting worse, but she couldn't stop typing. The more she wrote, the more questions came to her mind.

And what about the black car? Was it someone Lanie hired to scare them or was it Lanie herself?

The driver was rather dark. And she left the motel early. It's possible she could have followed us, could have rented a car. And was it Lanie who broke in here Sunday afternoon? She would have had time. But what was she looking for? It really comes down to what Christine had that could be used for blackmail. Had Christine told her she had hidden something in my house? That must be it. I guess it really doesn't matter now. With Lanie dead, whatever evidence Christine had against her may as well stay hidden. But what if it wasn't against Lanie? Is the killer still out there?

Fonnie rested her right hand on the keyboard. It was slow and laborious typing with just one hand. Her mind was telling her she had more to write, but she couldn't manage it now. Maybe later. But her brain wouldn't let her hand rest. She typed one more line.

No, the evidence cannot stay hidden. It's in this house. I know it is. I've got to find it.

Fonnie tried to put herself in Christine's mind. Where would be the best place to hide something? Depends on how big it was. It must have been small, small enough to be placed in her purse or coat pocket, small enough to bring in without being noticed. And it had to be somewhere that the Sunday intruder didn't think to look. In a kitchen drawer? Behind the canisters? Some place not frequently used or Keisha would have found it by now. Maybe she should wait for Keisha to come tomorrow and they could search together. Besides, she was too tired now. The search would have to wait.

Fonnie retreated to the recliner, made sure she had the remote and her phone, propped her feet up. She flipped on the TV but turned the volume down. She didn't mean to doze off, but apparently she did because the next thing she knew her telephone was ringing and the wall clock was close to three.

"Fonnie, have you heard?" It was Bebe's voice.

"Heard?" Fonnie tried to get her brain in gear, but it seemed to be stalled. It wasn't until she glanced at the TV and noticed the news anchor's lips moving, that she became alert. "About Lanie Franklin's suicide, you mean?"

"Yes, isn't it awful? Of course, she was a bitch, but I didn't think she was a murderer."

"Is that what they're saying?"

"No. But why else would she kill herself? The guilt must have been too much."

"That's what I was thinking too, but maybe we're jumping to conclusions. Brian says I have a tendency to do that. Maybe he'll have some more info when he gets home."

"Maybe. Has Dickson talked to you? He came into the bookstore this morning. But that was before they found Lanie's body."

"He talked to you? About yesterday?"

"Yeah, said you'd called and left a message. Something about someone trying to kill us. I told him I thought someone was just trying to scare us, or that it was just road rage." When Fonnie didn't say anything, Bebe went on, "He hasn't talked to you yet?"

"No, he hasn't. Why did he see you before coming to see me?" Fonnie was peeved. After all, Mike Dickson was *her* detective friend, not Bebe's. Didn't he appreciate her efforts to help? Didn't she deserve to have his attention? Why should she be delegated to second place? Fonnie swallowed her hurt pride and asked, "What was his take on our little adventure?"

"I don't really know. He's like a sponge. He soaks up information, but leaks very little of it himself."

"You just haven't learned the fine art of squeezing it out of him." And that's why, Fonnie reasoned, he didn't come to her first. He knew she'd get more out of him than he wanted to tell. He'd not get away with that again. One way or another, she'd find out everything about the murder investigation *and* with Lanie's death.

"Got to go, Fonnie. Some customers just came in. By the way, Neil called and asked me out to dinner tonight. You know, I haven't had an honest-to-goodness dinner date in ages. I'm not sure I remember how to act."

"I thought you were mad at Neil because he didn't show up for our weekend activities."

"I was, but he explained all that. I think I misjudged him. He's really a nice guy."

Sure, Fonnie thought, and I'm Mother Teresa. But she put a smile in her voice for Bebe's benefit, "So have fun tonight." Then she couldn't help adding, "But be careful."

Fonnie shook her head in bewilderment. Now why did she say that? She had no reason not to trust Neil. She hadn't even met the man—had never talked to him.

About the time Fonnie hung up the phone, she heard a knock on the door. She took her time getting there, and opened it to Tyrone's smiling face.

"Your yard man reporting for duty, ma'am."

"Wonderful. Come in and sit a spell."

"No. I'd better get right to work." Tyrone hesitated. "Fact is, I don't think your grandson likes me. I don't think he'd want me in the house."

"Nonsense. Brian was just upset Sunday when he met you. The break-in and all. You understand."

"Yes ma'am, but I do have lots of work to do. The city is supposed to pick up leaves this week so I'll get them to the curb."

Fonnie watched him as he tossed his rakes from the trunk of his car. Fine boy, she thought, a fine boy.

Later, when Brian came home, Fonnie was heartened to hear him call out a lively hello to Tyrone. Tyrone answered back, but kept on working. Fonnie thought that given time, the two young men would become friends.

Brian spread supper on the table, compliments of the Colonel. Fonnie let him get a head start on a chicken breast before she brought up her concerns about Lanie's death.

"Honestly, Gram, I don't know any more than you do about Ms. Franklin's death." Brian scooped another helping of KFC potato salad onto his plate. "I'm just a rookie, remember?"

"But you can nose around, ask questions, listen to the scuttlebutt."

"I do, but it is only scuttlebutt. I'm not privy to the facts."

"So I'll take what I can get. What is the grapevine saying?"

Brian sighed. "Rumor has it that her wound may not have been self-inflicted."

Fonnie dropped her biscuit and stared at Brian in

amazement. "No kidding. Actually, the thought crossed my mind, but I ignored it. I was thinking Lanie was too self confident, too assured of her place in the world to kill herself."

"Whoa there. This is nothing official, and don't you go blabbing about it to anybody."

"Of course not. But, you know, if it wasn't suicide, it puts a whole new light on the problem. When Christine was killed, I thought the perp was surely someone opposed to CATWAG and was sending them a warning. Now if Lanie was murdered, the perp might be someone on the other side of the fence."

"Perp?" Brian nearly strangled on his tea. "Where did you get that word?"

"Isn't that what you cops call the perpetrator? The malefactor? The felon? The bad guy?"

Brian couldn't stop laughing. "Yeah," he finally managed to say, "that's what we call the bad guy, along with a few other choice words." When he had control of himself, he went on. "But I think you're missing the point. If Lanie Franklin's death wasn't a suicide, but was made to look like one, then the perp was probably trying to place the blame for Christine's death on her and thus end the investigation. But like I said before, I really don't know anything official."

Fonnie spent the rest of the evening pondering what little she did know. What she lacked in facts, she compensated for with her gut feelings. Now she didn't doubt for a minute that Lanie had been murdered, and she felt sure the same person had committed both murders. But was the perp for or against the landfill? That was the knotty question.

Maybe tomorrow she and Bebe would have a chance

to bounce their ideas back and forth. Fonnie hoped that tonight, her friend was having a good time with Neil.

BEBE WANTED IT TO BE a fun evening. She vowed to herself to steer clear of any mention of CATWAG or the murder or the suicide. That left very few topics of conversation. She decided Halloween might be a good bet.

"Do you get many trick-or-treaters at your place?" she asked while smearing sour cream on her baked potato.

Neil shook his head. "Not too many kids in my apartment complex. And I'm not home anyway. The school dance, you know."

"That's right. You usually chaperone. My kids used to tell me how strict you were about not allowing anybody back outside once they came in. And how you made everyone remove their masks when they came in so you could identify them."

"That's right. I've been called "Vinegar Vincent" because I'm such a sourpuss."

That made Bebe laugh and she realized it was something she hadn't done lately. It felt good. "My kids didn't reveal that little tidbit, but if they had, I would have disagreed."

"Thanks." Neil's attention seemed to be completely on the roll he was buttering until he looked up and caught her gazing at him. "Would you like to go?"

"Go?"

"To the Halloween dance? I can bring a date. And I'm allowed to dance. I don't have to mind the door all the time."

"Sure. Sounds like fun." Bebe stopped her fork halfway to her mouth. "Do I have to wear a costume?"

"Absolutely. I'm going this year as a Vlasic Pickle.

You could go as a cookie or a donut and we could call ourselves "Sweet and Sour."

They spent the next several minutes trying to figure out how to make a donut costume. Bebe nearly doubled over at his suggestion that she wear a life preserver around her waist and decorate it with chocolate-colored crepe paper. "Enough already. Let's change the subject."

Neil sipped his tea, his face sober. "I didn't intend to bring this up, but I really want to know. About your accident yesterday—was it just road rage or could it have been something more sinister? When I heard the news today about Lanie Franklin, I got this eerie feeling again."

"Eerie feeling?"

Neil nodded his head. "A feeling of danger. This crazy business isn't over. Please tell me everything you know about the case."

And Bebe did. It was so nice to have someone to talk to—someone who cared about her—someone she could trust.

TWENTY

THE NEXT MORNING Keisha was bright and merry while Fonnie was pensive. "Worn out supervising Tyrone's yard work?" Keisha asked. "He seems to have done a lot yesterday."

"He sure did, and he doesn't need any supervision. He's a very hard worker."

"You two are getting to be good buds, aren't you?"

"If that means we're friends, then you're right. Tyrone is a fine boy. You ought to be proud of him."

"I am," Keisha said. "Very proud. Just like you're proud of your grandson."

Leave it to Keisha to say just the right thing, Fonnie thought. She *was* proud of Brian, but right now she was also a little perturbed. "You know he left this morning for a seminar in Raleigh—a two day seminar. He didn't even tell me until this morning."

"Oh. That means you'll be alone tonight. Does that worry you?"

"Of course not. He's a big boy. He can take care of himself in the big city."

"That's not what I meant and you know it. Does it worry you to be alone here at night?"

"No. Why should it?"

"It shouldn't. But if it does, I can arrange to sleep over."

"Poppycock. I lived alone for years after Harrison died." Fonnie grinned at Keisha. "And Brian told me he'd asked for a patrol car to do drive-bys here during the night. So you see, there's not a thing to worry about."

"Good. Now I'm ready for my marching orders. Any special cleaning you want me to do this morning?"

Fonnie set her coffee down. "No. No cleaning today. We're searching."

"Searching? For what?"

"I don't rightly know, but I'm convinced Christine hid something in this house—an envelope, a picture, a letter—something she was using for blackmail. We find it and we solve her murder and maybe Lanie's as well."

"Lanie Franklin? The news said she committed suicide."

"Maybe. Maybe not. I promised Brian I wouldn't talk about it. But just the same, I have my own ideas."

"So where do we start?"

Keisha tackled the kitchen while Fonnie dragged a stool to the china cabinet in the dining room. They pulled out every drawer, looked behind every dish. Keisha pulled out appliances from the wall. Fonnie stuck her hand inside sugar bowls and teapots and soup tureens. An hour later they had found nothing except dust and a few mouse droppings. Keisha insisted on stopping and cleaning up the mess. Then Fonnie shooed her to the living room to look under cushions, behind drapes, inside the family Bible. Still nothing.

"Now what?" Keisha asked.

"I don't think anyplace in the den has been missed. That is pretty much where the intruder looked the most, strewing papers all over. And when Brian and I put every-thing back we would have noticed something unusual."

"How about the bedrooms?"

"I've looked everywhere in mine. As far as I know,

Christine didn't go upstairs. I told her not to bother with Brian's room, and the other rooms aren't used. I suppose she could have gone up there to hide something."

"An unused room would be the first place I would hide something," Keisha said.

Fonnie nodded. "You may be right." She looked at the clock. "About time for you to go. Maybe you can check upstairs tomorrow."

"Want me to come back this evening and fix your supper? Maybe play a game of Parchesi?"

Fonnie was pleased with Keisha's concern, but she was determined not to show any apprehension about being alone. "That won't be necessary. There's leftovers, and I'm into a good book, so I won't be lonely. Thanks anyway."

After a quick supper, Fonnie huddled down in the recliner and turned on the evening news. The Big Story was Lanie Franklin's death. To Fonnie's surprise, the newscaster started with the very same scuttlebutt that Brian had mentioned—the death may not have been a suicide. The police had not confirmed nor denied it. But in her bones, Fonnie knew that Christine's murderer had struck again.

She may have fooled Keisha with her brave facade, but she hadn't fooled herself. With the coming of darkness, the fears she had shoved to the back of her brain came creeping out. It wasn't just fear of being alone, but the chilling thought that a killer was out there, somewhere, in the night. True, patrol cars would be going by her house, but was that real protection?

Thoughts flew in and out of her brain like lightning bugs on a black night, not staying long enough to be clearly examined. She headed for the computer. Maybe

I need to get something on paper. As she bent over the keyboard, the phone in her pocket knocked against the desk. Dang, she thought, this phone is going to break someday being banged around all the time. She took the phone out of her pocket and laid it by the computer.

She wanted to type what was on her mind, but nothing came out. Nothing made any sense. What she needed was a nice soothing cup of tea—in a genuine china cup—with a cookie on the side. Better than a tranquilizer anytime.

Fonnie took her cane and made her way into the dining room. She balanced on her good foot and reached one of the delicate teacups Amy had brought her from Venice. Her daughter had gone there on a class trip during her senior year in college. The cups had seldom been used through the years—only on special occasions: birthdays, holidays, welcoming new friends, saying goodbye to old ones. This afternoon while searching the cabinet, she had been reminded that she was a recipient of love. In times past the teacups had reassured her that her little world was safe and secure. She needed that reassurance tonight.

She placed the dainty cup and saucer on the narrow counter, studied their pale pink rosebuds, their soft lime-green leaves, their slender gold rims. Fonnie took a deep breath and waited expectantly for some succor, a little comfort to warm her chilled soul. It didn't come. She shrugged. "Okay, on to step two." She slipped the cup and saucer onto the tea tray, bypassed the empty silverware drawer. "Sorry about that," she said to the cup. "I know a fine china cup like you deserves a real silver spoon, but since mine were stolen, you'll have to be content with a silver-plated one."

Fonnie grasped her cane and started the journey across the dining room past the kitchen table, past the sink, to the microwave, pushing the tea cart as she went. All the time she carried on a conversation with herself or her cup or some beloved ghost that often visited her. "My next kitchen will consist of only a walkway with appliances on one side and bar stools on the other, and everything within easy reach."

She filled a small teapot with water from the tap, dropped in a *Lemon Zinger Green Tea* bag, placed it in the microwave, then retraced her steps to fish a teaspoon out of the drawer next to the sink.

As she did so, a tinkling noise echoed throughout the room. Must be the wind chime on the back porch, she thought.

She stood perfectly still and listened. But the wind wasn't blowing. She had noticed earlier when she'd pulled the drapes in the den that the few leaves still clinging on the trees were hanging like limp tissue paper. Not a bit of breeze hastened their descent. The leaves that Tyrone had raked the day before were still in perfect piles, waiting to be picked up.

Nothing was stirring at all in the darkness—except the wind chime.

Fonnie closed the drawer slowly, quietly. She froze in place. She could feel her pulse quicken, her knees weakening. Someone was on her porch—hidden in the darkness.

Brian had put the yard chairs away for the season, her few potted plants had been brought inside. There was nothing out there except the wind chimes—and whoever had bumped against them.

While she debated whether to turn on the porch light or not, the microwave beeped. She thought of Brian's suggestion to install an alarm system. She'd put him off, told him she would think about it. Why did she always have to be so doggone stubborn?

Fonnie willed herself to stay calm, to think rationally. The doors were locked and chains in place. Brian had learned it would be next week before the new window locks and protective grills could be installed so he'd nailed all the ground floor windows shut. She actually was quite safe. Or was she?

Whoever was on her porch had one advantage. He could see her because of the bright kitchen light, but she couldn't see out.

Fonnie knew she had to do two things. One, get out of sight and two, call for help. Neither action was going to be easy. She remembered she'd left the phone by the computer. She couldn't see the phone from where she stood and she didn't think it was visible through the window. Perhaps she could make her tea and carry it back into the next room and her visitor wouldn't even know she suspected anything. She pulled the tea cart near her, removed the pot from the microwave and placed it on the cart. Then she reached into the cookie jar and placed two shortbread cookies on a napkin next to the teacup. She smiled inwardly. That should reassure the visitor that she was completely unaware of him. Unless her trembling hands gave her away.

She pushed the cart carefully, her back to the kitchen door and window, forcing herself not to look back. As she exited the room, she snapped off the kitchen light. Nothing unusual about that. She never left lights burning in empty rooms.

Fonnie reached the den, slid the cart and herself to the right out of sight of the kitchen window and headed toward the phone.

The sound of breaking glass stopped her in her tracks.

TWENTY-ONE

FONNIE SCRUNCHED UP against the wall, made herself tiny, held her breath. She heard glass cascading against the sink and stove, heard grunts and curses, heard feet crashing on the floor, heard chairs being overturned. She let out a primal scream—then tried to collect her emotions and her thoughts. She reached behind her and flipped off the den light. The darkness was to her advantage. She knew the room, the intruder didn't. At least she hoped it wasn't someone who had been her guest.

Fonnie gauged the distance to the desk and her phone. Could she make it? Or should she slide down behind the big Morris chair? No, she wouldn't be able to hide for long. She propelled herself toward the phone forgetting that the tea cart was in front of her. Her cane hit the cart. She heard tea splash, dishes rattle, and her cane plummet to the floor. At the same time she heard footsteps coming closer.

Fonnie shoved the tea cart to one side, stepped as far as she could with her right foot and dragged the other one along. Another step, another drag. She was almost at the desk.

She could hear someone right behind her. She could smell stale cigarette smoke. She took one more step. She seized the phone. She punched the talk button. Her thumb slipped. She only had time to strike one number before the phone was slapped out of her hand. It landed on the floor and the intruder kicked it across the room.

An arm gripped her neck, snapped her head back, jarred her teeth and her brain. Her legs collapsed. Her body wanted to sink into the carpet, but the arm held her up, choking her, dangling her.

Then as suddenly as he had grabbed her, the man released his hold. Fonnie crumpled to the floor. She lay there, gasping, praying, planning. She could pretend to be unconscious and maybe he would leave her alone. Maybe he would steal whatever he'd come for and then go away. It didn't happen. The overhead light clicked on. He'd found the switch by the door. Fonnie kept her eyes closed, but the light seeped in under her lids.

He kicked her chin with his foot, and her eyes popped open. "Good. You're awake. Now just give me what I want and I won't hurt you."

Fonnie propped herself up on one elbow, rubbed her chin and her neck. "You've already hurt me, you big boob." She twisted around so she could see the face of the bastard who had attacked her. She planned to memorize every detail to tell the police. What she saw was a black ski mask showing only two smoldering dark eyes.

"Unfortunately, there's more where that came from," he said, "if you don't cooperate." He yanked her up by one arm, hauled her over to the desk chair, slammed her down. "Now, all I want is the picture Christine Hauner gave you. Hand it over, and I'll be gone." Fonnie was surprised at the sound of his voice. It was quite cultured, like a businessman or a teacher.

She kept staring at him. Maybe she couldn't see his face, but she would be able to describe his clothes and manner. He was a big man, five-ten or eleven, heavy but not fat. He wore jeans, a dark denim jacket, and black gloves. She glanced at his feet. From the kick on her chin, she figured he was wearing heavy boots. She was right.

Something about the set of his shoulders seemed familiar to Fonnie. She rubbed her chin again and an image skidded into her memory. "You're the man in the black car, the one who ran us off the road." She shook her head at him. She was determined not to let her fear show. "You could have killed us. Why in the hell did you do that?"

"Just following orders. Like now. Where's the picture?"

Fonnie knew the truth wouldn't get her anywhere, so why not tease him a little? "I burned it. I figured after Christine was dead, it wouldn't do anybody any good. So I burned it." Fonnie smiled. "So you can tell whoever hired you, that he doesn't have to worry about it any longer."

"I don't buy that story."

Fonnie didn't care if he bought it or not. All she was doing was buying time. Her call to 9-1-1 should be bringing help soon. When she first got back from the nursing home, Brian had programmed several numbers into her speed dial. He'd explained to her very carefully that in an emergency, she only needed to punch the number 1. That's what she'd done before her attacker knocked the phone to the floor. The connection was probably broken, but surely her address had made it to the dispatcher's monitor. She thought that even now she heard the faint sound of a siren. She needed to keep talking so he wouldn't hear it in time to get away.

"On second thought, maybe I didn't burn it. That might have been a different one. What kind of picture are you looking for? Maybe I do have it here somewhere."

The siren was definite now. Probably just turned on Mimosa Street, Fonnie thought. The cavalry will be here very soon.

The Ski Mask Man heard it too. "Damn." He bolted out of the room. Fonnie heard him rattle the chain on the kitchen door, heard it open and slam shut, heard his footsteps run across the porch.

"For a big man, he can move mighty fast," she said to herself. Fonnie bent down, picked up her cane, and made her way to the front door. She flipped on the porch light and welcomed the police.

They were the same two who had investigated her Sunday evening break-in. "Thank God, you're all right," Wally exploded. "When the phone cut off after your 9-1-1 call, the dispatcher thought the worst. What happened?"

Fonnie tried to tell them what had happened with a minimum of words and a maximum of gestures. "The back door. He ran that way." Wally followed her pointing hand to the kitchen while Dwayne called for backup. At the same time, an ambulance wailed to a stop in front of the house.

"What's that doing here? I don't need an ambulance."

"I'm not sure about that," Dwayne said. He guided her to the den sofa, told her to stay put. "We didn't know what we'd find, so they sent out all the troops. I'll send the fire truck back when it gets here, but the medics will have to examine you."

Fonnie lolled back. She was out of energy, out of breath, out of resistance. She let the nice EMT lady take her blood pressure, examine her for wounds, bring her a drink of water. "I think you'll be fine, but you shouldn't be alone. Is there someone I can call to stay with you?"

Fonnie gave her Keisha's number. "Tell her to take her time. I'm not going anywhere."

Dwayne came back into the room. "We've got men surrounding the neighborhood, but it isn't likely we'll nab the guy." He took out his notebook. "Now tell me exactly what happened. Everything you can remember. Then I need to call Brian. I know he's in Raleigh."

Fonnie scowled. "How do you suppose the intruder knew Brian wasn't here? Maybe you have a leak at the police department. Brian leaves town, and immediately his grandma becomes a prime target."

Dwayne rolled his eyes ever so slightly. "Mrs. Beachum. His car is gone. So he's not here. A logical conclusion."

"Oh, yeah." She gave him a silly grin. "I guess I'm not thinking too straight right now." She rubbed her jaw again. It still hurt—like a dull toothache. Maybe I ought to go to the dentist tomorrow, she thought. That brute may have jarred some teeth loose. She turned back to Dwayne. "Do you have to call Brian?"

"Yes." He gave a rueful smile. "If I didn't, he'd shoot me when he got home."

Fonnie nodded. "You're probably right." She recounted the happenings of the evening. "He probably wasn't in the house more than ten minutes, but it seemed like an eternity."

When she finished, Dwayne slowly closed his notebook. "At least now we know what he was looking for. I imagine Lieutenant Dickson will have a team out here in the morning to search for the missing picture."

Fonnie didn't tell him that she and Keisha had already searched the place. Apparently they hadn't done a thorough job.

With a squeal of brakes, a slamming door, and a hug that nearly smothered Fonnie, Keisha arrived. "I knew I should have come back over. I should have insisted. Oh, Fonnie, you look terrible. You're going to bed this very minute." She turned to the officer. "Are you through interrogating her?"

Dwayne raised his eyebrows at the dynamo that had just blown in. "I wasn't interrogating her. I was just taking her statement."

"Whatever. Is she free to go?"

"Yes," Dwayne said with a smile. "She's free to go, as long as she doesn't leave the house."

"The only place she's going is to bed." Keisha pulled Fonnie up, handed her the cane, started to lead her off. Then she turned back to the officer. "Can we assume you'll put a watch on the house for the rest of the night so we can get some sleep?"

"Yes ma'am. We already had a car patrolling the area. That's how we got here so quickly, but now we'll leave a car here all night. And, before you ask, we're already boarding up the broken window."

"Good!"

Fonnie was too tired to comment on Keisha's performance tonight. Tomorrow she'd tell her how proud she was. Of course, her aide had been taking lessons in assertiveness from an expert.

TWENTY-TWO

Bebe awoke on Thursday morning to the sound of rain sluicing across her bedroom window and wind battering her trash can. Neither had been predicted. She reached for the remote and switched on the local channel. She wondered how the perky weather girl would explain away the prediction of cold, clear, calm. Bebe shivered. Well, she got the cold part right.

The girl put the blame on a low pressure front that had veered off-course during the night. "But," she grinned as she patted her bouncy curls, "all this mess will clear out by noon, and the temperature will rise to the upper fifties."

"I wouldn't bet the ranch on it," Bebe murmured as she squirmed out of bed and snatched her robe. The weather girl disappeared along with her maps and low-pressure areas. Bebe was heading for the shower when the voice of the anchor man stopped her. "And now, to the supposed suicide of Myerson Corporation vice-president, Lanie Franklin. The police say they are investigating the case as a possible homicide."

Bebe flopped down on the bed and listened intently to the rest of the report. "Well, I'll be doggoned. Wonder if Fonnie has heard this." She glanced at the clock. Not too early to call. She knew Fonnie was an early riser.

A soft, unfamiliar voice answered the phone. "Yes?"

For a moment Bebe thought she might have dialed the wrong number. "Good morning. May I speak to Fonnie, please."

"May I ask who's calling?"

Bebe was even more puzzled. Does Fonnie have a secretary now? "Bebe Englehook."

"Oh yes, Bebe. We've never met, but I've heard a lot about you." Bebe smiled as the voice on the other end of the line changed from frosty to bubbly warm. "I'm Keisha Riggs, Tyrone's sister and Fonnie's aide. Fonnie's right here. I'll see if she feels like talking."

Feels like talking? In their short acquaintance Bebe had never experienced a time when Fonnie didn't feel like talking. What was going on?

"Good morning, Bebe. How are you?"

Fonnie sounded drained, fatigued. "I'm fine," Bebe answered. "How are you?"

"Okay. Now."

"What do you mean—now?" When Fonnie didn't answer right away, Bebe cut in. "Never mind. Let me talk to Keisha again." There was a long pause and Bebe was afraid Fonnie might have hung up. Then she heard a swishing noise as the phone was passed. Bebe didn't wait for Keisha to say anything. "What's going on there?"

Keisha explained the break-in as best she could and how she had come over to spend the night.

"Brian didn't come home?" Bebe asked.

"No. He wanted to, but his friend, one of the police officers, assured him he didn't need to. He's already called this morning, though, and he'll be home this afternoon." Keisha hesitated, lowered her voice. "The problem is, I have an important exam this afternoon and since I didn't get to study last night, I really need to do it this morning. But I don't want to leave Fonnie alone."

"Don't worry about it. I'm coming over."

FONNIE WAS PLEASED to see Bebe, but was worried about the bookstore.

"No problem," Bebe said. "I just put the 'remodeling' sign back up."

"You know, at some point you'll actually have to do some remodeling or your customers are going to get suspicious."

"Right. And I will as soon as I have the time."

Keisha had ushered Bebe into the kitchen where a fresh pot of coffee was brewing. "You're sure you don't mind staying until Brian gets home?" she asked Bebe.

"Not at all. You run along and study and do great on that exam."

"Thanks. I will. Or at least I'll try."

Bebe waved her out. "And tell Tyrone 'Hey' for me."

After Keisha had gone, Bebe refilled Fonnie's coffee cup and poured herself one. "Now. Out with it. Tell me about last night."

When Fonnie finished her story, Bebe got up and went around to give her a hug. Fonnie twitched as Bebe's hands touched her neck.

Bebe jerked back. "What?"

"That's where he grabbed me. It's pretty sore."

"The louse!"

"My sentiments exactly."

Bebe drained the rest of her coffee. "I can't just sit here. Isn't there something we can do while we wait for the cops' search team?"

Fonnie slowly nodded her head. "Maybe we can find the infamous picture before they get here."

"But you and Keisha have already looked."

"Yes, but she said something just before she left yesterday that made a lot of sense."

"And that was?"

"That an unused room would be the best place to hide something. She was thinking of one of the empty bedrooms upstairs, but the library down here is seldom used." Fonnie pointed to the hallway past the dining room. "It isn't really a library, just a storeroom where we keep old books and that Brian uses occasionally to watch his training tapes."

Fonnie's hands started to tremble as a memory swooped into her brain. "I remember one day I saw Christine come out of there. She looked flustered or worried or something. thought at the time she might have noticed the police videotapes, and they upset her. So I told her not to bother to clean in there anymore." Fonnie took a quick gulp of coffee. "But as I look back, I don't think she was cleaning. She didn't have a dust rag or a broom, or anything in her hands." Fonnie got up. "Come on. Let's get moving."

Bebe followed Fonnie through the dining room, across the hall, and into the tiny library. "Whew," she said, "and I thought my store was crammed. You must have saved every book you ever read."

"Books are like friends or family to me. I can't bear to part with any of them. I come in here once in a while and just look at the titles. I remember the stories, the people who inhabit the books, who gave them to me, even where I was when I read them. They're like a memory bank that I can draw on when I need a little lift." Fonnie shrugged. "I figured you'd understand. Not many people do."

"I understand. You're a true bibliophile. But enough of that. Let the search begin." Bebe stared at the shelves in front of her. "How tall was Christine?"

"What?"

"If I was in a hurry to hide something in here, I'd most likely go for a book at my eye level. So how tall was Christine?"

"Makes sense. I'd say she was about four or five inches taller than you."

"Then I'll start looking at the shelf above my eye level. But not on this side. I would go around to the shelves in back so that if someone opened the door, I wouldn't be seen." Bebe went around the end of the stack, down the other side, to the corner. "I'll start here and work my way up."

Fonnie began to feel left out. "And I'm supposed to stand here and watch you?"

"No. You sit at the desk. I'm going to place the big books there for you to flip through. The small books I'll be able to go through myself. Of course, it would help if we knew what size picture or envelope we're looking for."

For the next hour silence reigned in the library, broken only by the swish of pages, and explosive sneezes from noses not accustomed to so much close-up dust. Fonnie was the first to give in. "I need to wash my hands, and get a drink of water."

"Me too, but let me finish this one shelf. Be with you in a minute."

Fonnie had gotten out juice glasses and was in front of the refrigerator getting out orange juice when Bebe jiggled into the kitchen, her hands behind her back. Fonnie looked up. "There's a bathroom in the hall. You look like you're about to pee your pants."

Bebe grinned. She brought her left hand out and waved a white envelope in the air. "How much would you bid for this beautiful snapshot?"

Fonnie dropped the juice container on the table and slammed the refrigerator door. "You found it!"

Bebe pursed her lips. "I found a picture, but I don't know if it's the right one. It was in James's *Portrait of a Lady*. Doesn't look like much to me." She reached out to help Fonnie to the table. "Sit down before you fall down, and I'll show it to you."

Fonnie slid into the nearest chair. Bebe took the snapshot out of the envelope and laid it on the table.

Fonnie pushed her glasses back, picked up the picture. She looked at the picture, looked away, then brought her eyes back. A tear slid silently down her cheek. She closed her eyes, sniffed, looked back at Bebe.

"You know who they are, don't you?" Bebe asked.

Fonnie shook her head. "You mean, the people?"

"Of course, the people. What else is there?"

Fonnie smiled. "You tell me first."

"The old lady is Ed Whitehall's mother and the disheveled teenager is his grandson, Jerry. I saw them both when I was there about the memorial service."

"So that's it. Christine was blackmailing Jerry, and Ed was trying to protect his grandson by getting the picture back. That's why he was buttering up to me, trying to find out what Christine had told me or given me. And it had to have been Ed who hired the thug who broke into my house."

Bebe plopped into a chair, poured some juice, and

took a long swig before replying. "I don't get it. There's nothing incriminating about this picture. Just two smiling faces."

"Three."

Bebe snatched up the picture. "Where? Where's the other face?"

"Look at the top of the dresser behind Jerry and Mrs. Whitehall—next to the bottle of cologne."

"All I see is a bottle of pills and a figurine." Bebe sucked in a gob of air. "Oh, my Lord. It's a silver unicorn! You told me you had one stolen."

Bebe laid the picture down again in front of Fonnie. "That's your unicorn?"

Fonnie nodded.

"Are you sure?"

"I'd know Leopold anywhere. What I find hard to believe is that Ed Whitehall would go as far as hiring someone to run us off the road or have someone break into my house and threaten me."

"Sometimes people will do anything to protect their loved ones."

"Even if that loved one was a murderer?"

Bebe stared at Fonnie. "You think Jerry killed Christine over a unicorn?"

"To keep from being exposed as a thief."

"But if this was about stealing your silverware, what does it have to do with the landfill—with CATWAG?"

"I'm guessing it had nothing to do with the landfill. The body was dumped there as a ruse—to throw the police off the track."

"I guess you're right, and it sure worked." Bebe smiled at Fonnie. "So, you going to call Mike with the news, or do you want me to do it?"

Fonnie sipped her orange juice slowly. Her throat hurt and it was still painful to swallow. She took the time to organize her thoughts. "Neither," she finally answered.

"But we've solved the case."

"And I would like nothing better than to inform Detective Dickson of that, but this picture alone isn't enough. We have to get Leopold back. We have to go to the Whitehall house and get the evidence."

"Are you crazy? Ed might be home."

"Call his office. Tell his secretary you're interested in booking a honeymoon cruise and you must talk to Ed. If he's in the office, then he's not home, and we can go there safely."

Bebe giggled. "And where is this honeymoon cruise going?"

"Timbuktu or Kalamazoo. Who cares? Tell him to get all the material together today and then make an appointment for tomorrow. That way he'll have to stay in the office and work."

Bebe made the call, listened a few moments, then said, "Thank you. I'll try again tomorrow." She turned from the phone with a long face. "He's not in the office today."

"Oh, no," Fonnie said. "So he's home?"

A smile split Bebe's face and she clapped her hands. "No. He's out of town and not expected back today."

"Then what are we waiting for?"

"But what if the police come here to do their search while we're gone?"

"Then they'll just have to wait. I'm going to find Leopold." Fonnie dived into the hall coat closet and came out with her raincoat. Bebe already had the door open. Fonnie hesitated. "Wait. I can't go yet. I promised Brian

I would tell him anytime I left the house. He's probably on his way home right now. I'll call his cell phone."

Fonnie went back into the den to make the call. She smiled when she heard the words, "Leave a message."

Good, she thought, much better than talking to him. "Brian, just wanted to let you know that Bebe and I are going to visit Gladys Whitehall, Ed's mother. She gets lonely and can use some company. Be home soon."

It took some maneuvering for Fonnie to climb up into Bebe's truck, but she was determined nothing was going to stop her now from finding Leopold.

TWENTY-THREE

FONNIE WAS HAVING SECOND THOUGHTS by the time they arrived at Ed's house. She probably should have called Mike about finding the picture. But would he have realized its significance? Could the police have gotten a search warrant on that single piece of evidence?

Bebe pulled up to the curb, parked, and helped Fonnie out. Well, Fonnie thought, as long as we're here, we might as well go for it. Bebe rang the bell. The window in the top of the old-fashioned door gave a view of the hallway and the kitchen beyond. Fonnie saw a middle-aged woman with frizzy hair approach the door, look out, then open it.

"Good morning, Mrs. Pruitt," Bebe said. "Remember me? Bebe Englehook."

The woman studied her a moment, then smiled. "Of course. You're the one who did the memorial service for poor Christine. I'm sorry I wasn't able to make it, but Mr. Whitehall said he planned to go. What can I do for you?"

Bebe extended her right arm toward Fonnie. "I'd like you to meet Fonnie Beachum. You may recall she was Christine Hauner's other client."

Mrs. Pruitt acknowledged Fonnie with a slight nod. "Of course. Pleased to meet you."

Fonnie stepped forward and gave the housekeeper her special Sunday-go-to-meeting-smile designed to bestow a blessing on the recipient. "We came over to visit with Gladys. I know how time consuming her care must be for you."

"Not really. I just feed her breakfast and lunch. Her aide comes in the afternoon and does her personal care." Mrs. Pruitt motioned for them to come in. "You're welcome to see her. Some days she responds to people, and some days she doesn't."

Fonnie and Bebe followed Mrs. Pruitt to the end of the hall. Fonnie reached into her purse and brought out the snapshot. "Maybe she'll respond to this picture. Isn't the boy her grandson?"

Mrs. Pruitt glanced quickly at the photo and smiled. "Jerry's her *great*-grandson. She loves that boy. See how she's grinning? She always knows when Jerry's around."

Fonnie pointed to an object in the picture. "That's rather an unusual figurine. I wonder where she got it."

"Jerry gave it to her. He's such a thoughtful boy. But come to think of it, I haven't seen it lately. I don't know what might have happened to it."

Fonnie felt her heart tumble down to her shoes. Had Ed destroyed Leopold to get rid of evidence? Her hands began to tremble.

Bebe took the picture and nudged Fonnie toward the open bedroom door. "Let's go on in and pay our respects to Mrs. Whitehall."

Fonnie nodded. The snapshot had reignited her hopes of getting Leopold back. She couldn't give up now.

Mrs. Pruitt led them in and introduced the visitors. Gladys Whitehall's frail body was propped up with pillows, one hand dangled over the side of the bed, and her vacant eyes stared into space. Fonnie's eyes went to the dresser. It definitely was the same one as in the

picture. And like the picture, the top held a box of
tissues, a bottle of cologne, an antique jewelry box, a
bottle of pills, and a black-eyed panda bear wearing a
pink beret. But no unicorn. No Leopold. She tapped
Bebe on the arm. "Let me have the picture."

Fonnie went over to the bed. She picked up the cold,
dangling hand and rubbed it gently. "Gladys, I came to
visit you because Christine was my friend also. You
remember Christine?" The old woman's features didn't
change, but Fonnie detected a tiny flicker of her eyelids.
"Of course, you remember her. You remember a lot of
things. You just have a hard time telling people about
them." Again, slight lifts of her eyelids. Now Fonnie was
warming to her mission. Twenty or thirty years slipped
away and she was back in the hospital, coaxing patients
out of comas, talking to the brain-damaged as if they
really understood her—sometimes eliciting a tiny smile
or even a word.

She held the photo of in front of the old woman.
"Here's a picture of you and Jerry. He's such a nice boy.
I know you're proud of him." One corner of the invalid's
mouth bent upward. "Does Jerry bring you presents a
lot? I know he loves you and wants you to have pretty
things." Fonnie pointed to Leopold in the middle of the
picture. "That's a beautiful little unicorn. Did Jerry give
you that?"

The old woman's smile widened. "Ummm," sneaked
through her dry lips.

Fonnie reached for a glass of water that sat on the
bedside stand. She positioned the straw in Gladys's
mouth. "Want a sip of water? It'll make you feel better. I
know you want to talk to me about Jerry. Such a fine boy."

Gladys swallowed, gave a slight nod.

Fonnie felt a resurgence of hope just as Mrs. Pruitt interrupted. "She seems to like you. Would you mind if I run out to the post office for a few minutes? I really need to get my sister's birthday gift mailed. I won't be gone long."

Bebe answered quickly. "No problem. We'll stay until you get back."

"Take your time," Fonnie added. She waved the housekeeper out and turned her attention back to Gladys.

Out of the corner of her eye, Fonnie noticed Bebe cautiously looking through the dresser drawers. She tried to ignore her as she carried on her one-sided conversation. "Did you like the unicorn? I bet you enjoyed looking at it on the dresser. Is that why Jerry put it there? So you could watch it?" This time the faded eyelashes definitely blinked. "But he's not on the dresser now. I wonder what happened to him. Did Jerry take him away?" No response. "Did Ed take him?" Not a movement.

Fonnie's heart thudded with disappointment. Would she ever see Leopold again? And even more important, would they find the evidence that might pin down the burglars—and maybe point to the murderer? She took a deep breath and went on. "Did Christine take him?" A slight nod and a hint of a smile. So Christine had hidden Leopold—probably to keep him safe from Ed and Jerry. But where? Did Gladys know? Fonnie's nerves were being stretched to the breaking point and her back was hurting, but she couldn't give up. "Bebe, could you bring me a chair? I need to sit a spell."

Bebe brought the chair and Fonnie made herself comfortable. She again took the frail hand in hers. "Christine took the unicorn to keep him safe. Is that right?" This time both corners of the woman's mouth turned up. She's actually enjoying this, Fonnie thought. It's probably the most attention she's gotten in months.

Fonnie knew her next question was really out in left field, but she had to try. "Gladys, do you know where Christine hid the unicorn?" The nod was accompanied by a guttural sound coming from deep in the woman's throat. Fonnie sat up straight, her energy and her hopes renewed. "Do you want to tell me where it is?" Another grunt. Oh boy, Fonnie thought. What do I do now?

She looked around at Bebe. Her friend gave her two thumbs up. "Go for it."

Fonnie turned back to her job. She decided she'd have to play a combination game of twenty questions and hide-and-seek. "You're doing great, Gladys. I really appreciate your help. Now I'm going to name different places where the unicorn might be hiding and you blink your eyes if I'm getting warm." A slow eye blink encouraged her to go on. First Fonnie ascertained that Leopold was indeed in the room. Then she chanted the names of the different pieces of furniture: the rocking chair, the chest of drawers, the bookcase. No response. She looked around the room to see what she might have missed when she heard a noise like a low yawn. Fonnie twisted around quickly. The old woman had her mouth partially open. Fonnie patted her bony arm. "I know you want to tell me. We'll keep trying. Is the unicorn near you?" Gladys's lips closed and she emitted a squeak.

Bebe had been standing still all this time, not making a sound. Now she moved closer to Fonnie and whispered, "She keeps looking at the dresser."

Fonnie frowned. "But you've already searched the dresser." She took up her position again, leaned closer to the old woman. "Is the unicorn hiding on your dresser?"

A long "ummmm" slid past the invalid's lips and her eyelids did a little dance.

Fonnie shoved her chair back, got up, moved to the dresser. She touched the top drawer and then looked back toward the bed. Gladys Whitehall shook her head ever so slightly. The same thing happened to the other two drawers. Fonnie's hand went back to the top of the dresser. Her fingers inched over to the tall jewelry box. Fonnie had one very similar to it.

The small drawers in front held rings and bracelets and the doors on either side pulled open to hold necklaces. "The unicorn is in here?"

"Ummm," came from the direction of the bed.

Fonnie snatched open the left side door, ran her fingers through dull gold chains and strands of pearls. None of them looked expensive. She reached behind, but she found nothing.

"She's still looking at it," whispered Bebe. "Try the other side."

The right side door seemed to be jammed and Fonnie gave it a hefty jerk. When the door opened, a seashell necklace came tumbling out. In the back of the box Fonnie saw a piece of yellow nylon fabric wrapped around an object.

Fonnie held her breath as she took the fabric out and carefully unfolded the layers of material. Her hands touched cold metal, and she lifted up a tarnished, but intact, silver unicorn.

She brought it to her lips, brushed back her tears. She held the unicorn high so Gladys could get a good look. "Thank you. You did good."

"Ummm"

"You rest now. I've got to make a phone call."

Gladys sighed, closed her eyes, and seemed at peace.

Bebe rushed over. "Are you positive it's yours?"

Fonnie pointed to the engraving on the bottom. *Fonnie, Number One.* "It was my husband's gift for our first anniversary."

Leopold held them mesmerized until Fonnie heard footsteps in the hallway and looked up. She saw the barrel of the gun before she saw who was holding it.

TWENTY-FOUR

"So you found the cussed thing. Swell." Ed White-hall kept the gun steady on Fonnie. "Jerry's been looking for it. Give it to me." Fonnie's mind was having trouble taking in exactly what was happening. "You're supposed to be out of town," she said.

"I was. Just got back. And in the nick of time."

Bebe stepped forward and tried to push Fonnie behind her. "Just in time to do some heavy explaining. What is Fonnie's unicorn doing in your house?"

Ed laughed. "You're the ones who need explanations. You come in here, threaten my mother, steal her belongings. What's the big idea?"

"This unicorn was stolen from my house along with my silverware. But you know all that. Your grandson is a thief, Ed, and a murderer. You've been trying to protect him." Here Fonnie's voice took on a softer tone. "I know you love Jerry, but turning him into the police may be the best thing you could do for him. He's young. He probably didn't know what he was doing. The courts will go easy on him. He'll have a chance to start over."

"Yeah," Ed said. "He might have a chance to start over."

Ed glanced over at his mother. Gladys Whitehall was staring at him in horror. He smiled at her. "It's all right, Mother, I'm not going to hurt them—or Jerry. But I do have to go away for awhile." He kept the gun trained on the two women as he quickly bent down and kissed his mother on the forehead.

He then waved the gun toward the hallway. Bebe and Fonnie moved in that direction. When they were out of the room, Ed reached back and closed the door.

"You two are pretty smart, but you've got it wrong. Jerry's no murderer. And I didn't do it to protect him. I had to protect myself."

Bebe gave a choking sound. "You killed Christine? And Lanie?" She took two quick breaths. "And now you're going to kill us?"

Fonnie's mind was whirling. She clenched Leopold in one hand and her cane in the other. She did her best to keep from trembling and to keep her voice calm. "And then what? Leave Jerry to take the rap? And leave your mother all alone?"

"The state will take care of mother, and like you said, Jerry can start over. But I can't. He and a buddy did the burglaries, but I set them up. My businesses were on the edge of bankruptcy. I had to find some way to get cash. Christine figured it out. At first she was willing to share in the loot. Then something happened to change her mind. She wouldn't listen to reason. But I'm betting you will. Killing the pair of you would serve no purpose. I'll lock you in the basement, give myself a few hours to get away. By the time you tell your story, I'll be out of the country. One advantage of being in the travel business is that my passport is always ready."

Ed backed away from them and opened a door at the far end of the hall. He motioned them with the gun.

"You won't get far," Bebe said. "Mrs. Pruitt will be back soon and let us out. The police will be on your tail in record time."

"Mrs. Pruitt already came back. I met her outside as I came in. I told her to take the rest of the day off—go to a movie—go shopping—even gave her fifty bucks. She won't be back for hours. And as soon as you're locked up, I'll call the agency and cancel Mother's aide." Again Ed waved the gun. "Now get down those stairs. If I have to shoot, I will."

Fonnie glanced to her left and saw a figure of a man through the glass of the front door. His face was obscured by the door facing. It wasn't until he turned slightly that Fonnie recognized Brian. Her brain started somersaulting. What was he doing here? He was in civvies. Did he have his gun with him? Could he see Ed's gun? Should she try to warn him?

She froze as she saw the door handle turn. Bebe tugged at her sleeve. "Come on, Fonnie. Let's do as he says."

Fonnie edged her way toward the cellar door, pretended to stumble and then righted herself. She had to keep Ed's attention on her and away from the opening front door. Bebe took two steps down, then she turned to offer Fonnie a helping hand. When she did, she stiffened, and let out a low, "Oh."

At the same time the hinges of the aged door creaked. Ed spun around. Brian vaulted into the hallway. Ed fired.

Brian clutched at his left arm, but the same time he hurled himself at Ed and the gun. The gun fired again. Fonnie heard glass shatter, and heard herself scream. Brian lay crumpled on the floor. Ed was part way up.

Fonnie swung her cane furiously at Ed's knees. He buckled and went down. Bebe jumped him from behind. She grabbed for his gun hand. Ed tried to shake her off, but before he could, Fonnie shuffled closer and attacked his face with Leopold's sharp hooves.

Ed dropped the gun to protect his eyes. Bebe pounced on his chest, reached up and slammed his head against the floor.

Fonnie used her cane to scoot the gun down the hallway. "Your phone," she yelled at Bebe. "Where's your phone?"

Bebe motioned with her head to her purse that laid on the stair step. Fonnie scrambled over Ed's feet and legs. She dropped Leopold and grabbed the purse, dumping it upside down. She snatched the phone as it started to slide down the stairs. She punched 9-1-1 and shouted, "Officer down! Officer down! 514 High Street. The Whitehalls."

Ed, who outweighed Bebe by at least fifty pounds, managed to push her off. Bebe's head cracked against the stairway door. Ed started crawling toward the gun.

Brian stirred and tried to sit up. Fonnie lurched around Bebe and stumbled over to him. Tears clouded her eyes as she attempted to stanch the flow of blood with her own hands. Brian moaned, opened his eyes, looked over Fonnie's shoulder. He shoved his grandmother aside and staggered up.

Fonnie stared in terror as Ed's hand grasped the gun. Before Ed had a chance to take aim, Brian lunged at him. With his left arm dangling uselessly at his side, Brian managed to bring his right hand up and landed a punch on Ed's jaw. Ed tottered, but he didn't fall. Brian did.

Bebe backed into the kitchen, snatched a chair, raised it up, and smashed it over Ed's head. This time Ed hit the mat.

Sirens wailed. Blue uniforms bolted up the porch steps. Fonnie flung herself over Brian's fallen body and sobbed.

TWENTY-FIVE

KEISHA WAS COMBING Fonnie's hair late Friday morning when Lieutenant Dickson called and said he'd be over with some information. "Could you tease my hair up a little more?" Fonnie said. "I think it makes me look younger."

"Honey, looking younger is a tall order. Let's just try for suave."

"Suave will do. But hurry. And I hope Bebe gets here soon. She said she was closing the bookstore and coming over. She'll want to hear what Mike has found out."

"What about Brian?"

"They're releasing him from the hospital this morning. Wally was going to pick him up. They should be here soon." Fonnie grimaced "Oh, Keisha, it was so horrible, seeing him there, nearly bleeding to death. We mustn't ever tell Amy how close a call he had. She worries about him all the time as it is."

A rap sounded at the door, but before Keisha got there, Bebe dashed in, tossed her jacket at the hall coat tree, brushed back her frizzled hair. "So tell me the latest."

"I don't have the latest yet," Fonnie said, "but Mike does and he'll be here shortly. Sit down, put your feet up, relax."

Brian and Wally came in the kitchen door about the

same time Mike knocked at the front. They met in the den and shook hands. "Heard you had yourself quite a time yesterday," the detective said.

"Guess so. I don't remember much after the first shot." Brian eased down into the Morris chair. He was careful not to bump the sling that cradled his left arm.

Fonnie went over to him and gave him a kiss on the cheek. "My hero. You risked your life for me."

Brian shook his head. "I'm no hero. I just happened to stumble into a big mess."

"Why were you at Ed's, anyway?" Mike asked. "Your grandmother told me why she was there, but not you. Did you suspect him of being involved?"

"Shucks, no. I thought Ed was an all right guy. The only reason I was there was to pick up Gram and maybe take her and Bebe out for lunch." Brian squirmed into a more comfortable position. "Gram had left a message on my cell phone that they were going over to visit Mrs. Whitehall. No problem there, I thought. Then when I got home and she wasn't here yet, I figured it would be a nice surprise if I met them there and we'd go somewhere and do lunch.

"It wasn't until I got up on the porch and looked through the window, that I knew something fishy was going on. But before I could get a handle on the situation, Ed saw me and blasted a hole through my arm. I think I fainted right about then." Brian chewed his bottom lip for a second, then looked back at Mike. "Heros aren't supposed to faint, are they?"

Mike laughed. "It's what you did when you came to, that falls into the hero category."

"Too bad I can't remember it."

Keisha brought in coffee and Danish for everyone.

"Mind if I stay on?" she asked. "No classes today. I finished my midterms yesterday."

"Fine with me," Fonnie said. "Mike?"

"Sure. No problem. Everything I tell you will be on the news before long."

Fonnie waved Keisha to sit and turned to the detective. "So. Tell us."

Lieutenant Dickson settled back, crossed one leg over the other. "Ed Whitehall isn't talking."

"But he practically confessed to Bebe and me that he did both the killings. Won't that stand up in court?"

"We'll get to that later." Mike flip-flopped his legs, ran his hands through his hair. "As I said, Ed wasn't talking, but Jerry couldn't blab fast enough. We picked him up at school and he actually seemed relieved. The story he told made his grandfather look like a second Fagin."

Wally and Brian both looked puzzled. "Sir," Wally said. "Who's Fagin?"

Mike waved his hand. "Just a literary allusion."

"A Charles Dickens character," Bebe said, "who trained a gang of boys to be thieves."

Brian shook his head. "And I thought Ed was a nice guy."

Mike went on. "Several months ago, Ed talked Jerry into doing the break-ins. He told Jerry he needed money desperately in order to continue to care for his mother. The boy claims he didn't want to do it, but felt he had to for his great-grandmother's sake. Jerry said his grandfather taught him how to break into empty houses, told him just to steal silverware, jewelry, small valuables that could easily be pawned. Jerry said he didn't want to work alone, so Ed approved him getting a sidekick.

He ratted his partner out the first thing and we picked the boy up at school also. He's just thirteen—bad home situation—desperate for money and attention."

Fonnie noticed Keisha swiping a tear. "What will happen to them?"

"Juvenile court. They'll both probably be tried as juvies. Maybe they'll serve enough time to make a good impression on them. Hope so, anyway."

"You said they broke into empty houses," Brian said. "How did they know?"

"That's where Ed showed his brilliance. Being in the travel business and in real estate, he had a two-pronged network. He knew when his clients would be cruising to the Bahamas or trekking over Europe. He would also know vacant houses for sale or for rent." Mike turned toward Fonnie. "In going through his office files, we saw where your daughter had consulted him about the possibility of renting this house out while you were in the nursing home."

Fonnie gasped. "Amy never told me anything about it."

"She was doing it for you, Gram," Brian said. "She knew your savings were running low."

"Of course." She cleared her throat and tried to get her mind back on crime. "So Ed lined up the empty houses for Jerry and his buddy?"

"That's right. Jerry said he couldn't refuse. You know his parents are dead, and Jerry is dependent on Ed. And it seems that Ed told Jerry his business was near bankruptcy. Jerry's crazy for his great-grandmother and thought he was doing the crimes to help her. So the boys did the dirty work, brought the loot to Ed, and he carried it to his fence in Atlanta."

"But Jerry decided to keep Leopold," Brian said.

When Mike gave him a blank look, he went on quickly, "The unicorn. Gram named him Leopold."

"Right. Jerry said he would often keep some of the trinkets he stole to give to his great-grandmother."

Bebe wiggled around on the sofa. "But all this still doesn't connect with Christine."

Mike nodded. "I'm getting to that. Jerry said Christine brought her camera to work one day and wanted to take a picture of him and Mrs. Whitehall. She insisted he sit in front of the dresser. He didn't realize until later that she wanted to be sure to get the unicorn in the picture. Jerry didn't think anything more about it until a few days later when Ed screamed at him. Wanted to know where he'd gotten that damned silver thing. Jerry didn't understand why Ed was so mad until he yelled about the bitch trying to blackmail him. Then Jerry said his grandfather muttered something about taking care of her sorry ass."

"Ohmygawd." Keisha shivered and moved her chair closer to the sofa where Fonnie sat.

"Jerry declares he doesn't know what happened to Christine, but he conceded that his grandfather may have killed her or possibly had Archie Clark do it."

Brian stirred. "Who's Archie Clark? I haven't heard of him before."

"He was Ed's fence, and I guess you could call him a hatchet man. Jerry reported seeing him around their house this week. Jerry had met the man when he went with Ed to Atlanta one time to deliver some stolen goods, but he'd never seen him here until this week. The Atlanta police have picked him up and we'll extradite him. He admitted to being your attacker, Mrs. Beachum. He was also the driver of the car that drove you and Mrs.

Englehook off the road. He said it was a rental car, so we'll be able to locate it and match the paint we found on the car you were in."

"But why?" Bebe asked.

"He says Ed forced him into it. And he claims that Ed did both killings. I think he may be ready to turn state's evidence in return for leniency. We'll probably be able to work something out."

"I hate to put a damper on things," Brian said, "but unless Clark has some evidence about the murders, we only have his word that Ed is the culprit."

Mike smiled. "Oh, we have more than that." The detective leaned back in his chair and made a steeple with his fingers.

Fonnie nearly bit her tongue to keep from shouting out at him. She knew he was enjoying keeping his audience in suspense, and she didn't really begrudge him the pleasure.

Finally the detective continued. "We know Mrs. Hauner was killed at her home. Blood on the carpet, and so on. Therefore we know her body was moved to the landfill site, probably in the trunk of someone's car." He paused again, this time for only a couple of seconds. "I just got the report on Ed's trunk."

Fonnie held her breath waiting for his next words. "He'd done a good job cleaning it out, but not good enough. We found hair that matched hers, some blood, and some fibers from the carpet in her house. Of course, the report is preliminary, but I don't doubt we'll have enough to convict Ed Whitehall on that murder. We're still at the beginning with the Franklin case, but give us time, and I think we'll tie it all together."

Fonnie fidgeted around trying to get more comfortable. She wanted to stretch out on the sofa, but Bebe was sitting on the other end. She compromised by propping her right leg over the bottom rung of Keisha's chair. "So that's the facts. Now how about filling us in on what you think the actual scenario was. Start with Christine taking the picture. I can understand that she probably thought the unicorn was from my collection. I remember her staring at the remainder of my collection one day and I told her about my missing Leopold. Do you think that's when she planned to blackmail Ed?"

"If you want conjecture, I'd say yes. She confronted him with the picture, saying she knew Jerry had stolen it and asked for money to keep quiet. I don't know if she suspected he was behind all the burglaries or not. Ed agreed, paid her a great deal of money, probably thought that was the end of it. But then Mrs. Hauner visited her daughter's grave, and perhaps changed her mind. She blamed the Myerson Corporation for her daughter's death, and since Whitehall supported Myerson, she may have decided he was guilty also."

"Sounds reasonable," Bebe said. "Maybe after her visit to the grave, Christine decided she wanted revenge more than money."

Mike nodded. "At any rate, I think when she got home she called Ed Whitehall, told him the deal was off—maybe she said she was going to the police with her evidence. He drove out to her house to change her mind and get the incriminating picture. Probably a struggle ensued. He may not have meant to kill her. When he realized what had happened, he had to get rid of the body. What better place than the landfill site? With the scheduled protest rally, the murder would naturally be connected to the controversy. He put the body where it would easily be found. Even stuck her billfold in her pocket so she could be identified. His plan was to confuse the police. And he did a good job of that. Having Clark follow you and Bebe to Virginia might have been another subterfuge to focus your attention on Myerson."

"But," Fonnie said, "he was still nervous that the picture would surface. Maybe Christine told him she'd hidden it here before he killed her. He probably broke in here himself on Sunday after the memorial service."

Brian leaned toward her. "But how did he know you wouldn't be home?"

"I guess that was my doing," Bebe said. "I told him she was going to my house after the service."

Keisha had said little during the proceeding, but she'd been listening carefully. "I still don't see why he murdered Ms. Franklin. How does she fit in?"

"Again I'm guessing," Mike said, "but he may have thought he could put a closure on the Hauner murder investigation. He and Lanie Franklin had worked closely to get approval for the landfill. If he called her, gave her some reason to meet him at the site, she wouldn't hesitate to do so. He met her, shot her, tried to make it look like suicide, so the police would think she had killed Christine and then couldn't cope with her guilt."

"What made you decide it wasn't suicide?" Brian asked.

"We questioned it in the very beginning because women seldom shoot themselves in the head. Then the angle of the shot wasn't quite right. We're still working on it. But when the media got wind that it may have been murder and broadcasted it, Ed might have panicked. He realized the Hauner case wasn't closed after all and that the damning picture might still come to light. That's when he sent Archie Clark in to scare the information out of Mrs. Beachum."

Bebe reached over and patted Fonnie's arm. "I still get the creeps when I think of that brute's arm around your neck."

"Yeah, and his boot on my chin." Fonnie pointed her finger at the detective. "I hope you guys don't let him off too easy."

"Don't worry about that. He has a lot to answer for." Mike got up, stretched. "Well, people, that's about it for now. We still have a lot of work to do, so I'd better get to doing it." Brian walked him to the door.

Bebe got up also. "Time for me to go too. Got an appointment to get my hair done." She did a little two-step on her way to the door. "Neil's taking me to the Halloween dance. We're going as Antony and Cleopatra."

EPILOGUE

FONNIE PEERED OUT the kitchen window, admired the new paint job on the back porch—Tyrone had become her handyman as well as her yard man. She studied the darkening sky. The clouds looked suspiciously like snow clouds. Fonnie wasn't against having snow on Thanksgiving—it would add to the holiday decor, but she hoped it wouldn't come until Amy and Paul were safely here. She smiled at the thought of finally meeting her daughter's gentleman friend. She was prepared to like him and thought Brian was also. He and Paul had spoken on the phone on a couple of occasions and seemed to hit it off.

She turned from the window and walked toward the computer with barely a limp. Fonnie had been diligent in doing her exercises, cheered on and bullied on by Keisha. Her walking had greatly improved. She still used her cane when going outside, but didn't need it in the house. She placed both hands on the keyboard. The fingers of her left hand were becoming stronger also, and her typing speed was increasing.

Instead of a date, she typed Thanksgiving Eve. She thought for a few moments, naming in her head the many things she was thankful for.

I'm so thankful the mess of last month is behind us now. Archie Clark admitted to getting the gun that killed Lanie Franklin for Ed, but he claimed he had no idea Ed would use the gun to kill someone. Mike says that the case against Ed is now complete. He'll be tried for both murders, for multiple thefts, and for contributing to the delinquency of minors. Archie will spend several years in jail for receiving stolen goods, for breaking and entering, for assault.

Tyrone visited the two boys in the juvenile home and said he thinks they'll do all right. They just need the right guidance now.

Gladys Whitehall seems content at Springwillow. She likes the ceramic unicorn I gave her. He sits on her dresser top. It's a musical one and the nurses wind it up for her.

Myerson Corporation withdrew their application to build the landfill, stating that the citizen opposition and Ms. Franklin's death made it difficult to carry out their mission. Groverton still needs a new landfill, and the county is taking bids. But Bebe and CATWAG will make sure safety considerations come first.

Bebe remains a good friend. She and Neil are dating on a regular basis, and she seems really happy. She decided to trade her truck for a comfortable Ford Escort. She took me out to lunch and to a CATWAG meeting last week.

Brian's arm has completely healed. He'll finish his rookie training by the end of the year and will be a full-fledged officer of the law. I'm so proud of him.

And finally, there's Amy and Paul. I think

*something serious is developing between them,
and I'm glad.*

It's going to be a wonderful Thanksgiving Day.

Fonnie clicked the print icon, leaned back in the desk
chair. Her eyes lit on the shelf holding her unicorn collection. She got up, went over to the shelf, picked up the
silver figurine on the bottom shelf. She rubbed her
fingers over the inscription on the bottom. *Fonnie,
Number One.* She heard a car door slam. She smiled,
kissed Leopold's horn, and gently replaced him in his
place of honor.